2 Those Who Don't 4get

By

Jermar Jerome Smith

THE INTRODUCTION

Before entering this story I feel at least it's right for you all to know that this one means dear to me. And does has some sentimental value apart of it when writing it because it reflects real situations, real individuals, and in fact real children whom are no longer here basking in their lives and fulfilling everything they were suppose to accomplish while here. Based on some strange occurrence that found it's way in their lives that I feel wasn't ordained and I definitely don't feel was an act of life at all. Coming straight into this after finishing "Shawty" I was heavily frustrated with the case in regards to the Kendrick Johnson death. For those who don't know he was a teenager found dead in a Georgia school to which he attended With his body rolled in fitness mats for some unknown reason. That the media failed to accurately expressed what it is that truthfully occurred. Honestly hearing it turned me to all the suspicions that point directly to the actual situation which was nothing other than organ harvesting. Why is that one might would say ? It is because although knowing the market for that activity is majorly silenced as to happening before our eyes everyday that many of us intend to look the other way on or just aren't connected mentally to analyze. When they did the autopsy (or when they finished) on this well active boy who also suited on the basketball team, please with no exaggeration people many of his vital organs were all missing. Even more gutless and heinous by the muthafuckas they had the inhumane nerve to substituted this young man's source parts with newspaper. Now just imagine your child or anyone for that matter that your close to being found like this. With no answers or real explanation unveiled especially from the piece of shit ass police who suppose to being doing the investigation as to what they're paid for. Not just for whites and others but all people. Unfortunately that come to past and since 2013 when this case surface we haven't yet seen the truth and I guarantee we never will based off none of us actually being there in the moment.

To make things even more worst than worst. Having being that I finally completed the final draft to this story. Only but a couple months passing there was yet another situation no different than Kendrick's that occurred. Only this time a young beautiful girl who had fallen victim this time around. Her name was Kenneka Jenkins. She was nineteen and attending a party with some friends, had too much to drink as any young person would and according to Chicago police and obvious edited surveillance cameras this no more than hundred pound girl stumbled herself intoxicated inside a hotel refrigerator and froze herself to death. It didn't take no more than a couple hours for the story to break leaving all kinds of theories and false speculations as to her death foretold. But yet again I could only speak my personal perspective on the disheartening situation and it also leading directly to organ harvesting as well. Garnering my proof from a little old video where female worker whom worked inside the hotel's kitchen that shattered the media's story completely. Displaying how it was downright impossible for her to land in that freezer or in fact open it by her self.

My final point in the opening to this story, as Kenedrick and Kenneka aren't the only ones subjected to this haunting reality. The same with the lost d.c girls, Sandra Bland, and millions of others. I just want my people to know. Please be careful, understand the times that you are in, parents I need you to teach your kids about this structure as it has it out for them and will do any and all as to bring them to victimization without any justice as to explaining to you, and always be alert, I repeat ALWAYS BE ALERT. Even with so called friends. There's people out here who don't just want sex, who don't just want slaves, they want your internal parts as well and are willing to pay an unbelievable amount of money for them. I love you all and care about you dearly otherwise I wouldn't tell you this or write this story. So please endure and enjoy. And more than anything BE CAREFUL. PEACE (TWO FINGERS TOGETHER).

The sound of the ambulance sirens racing are in the cold distance. When the blaring gets much louder like a signal for an arrival. A hard shot like metal slamming through wood is heard. Incoming a hospital entrance in a panic hurry is a team of paramedics navigating a gurney to the emergency ward. Propped on to the stretcher as it rolls through the medic doorways housing the harmed of patients that occupy them. Is a mature man with his shirt ripped open blinking in and out of consciousness. Accompanied behind the paramedics as they scream in emergency " This man needs help immediately or we're going to lose him". Is the man's wife and son. His only offspring with his hand locked on to his, he assures his injured father with words of comfort " you fight it, you fight it." His wife looks on in tears touching his face like it could be her last time. In the man eyes of worry is a gateway to his mental, his point of vision. While there he sees his fear of dying leaving behind his wife Daisy of thirty plus years and his only living heir to his next generation of life, his one and only son ALEX. The weakening man thinks of all he'll leave behind once he's past into the after life. Setting sail with his darling wife DAISY on their expensive yacht watching the sunset across the beauties of the water like they always dreamed and discussed after his retirement. Or spending valuable time as a grandfather tossing around a football in the backyard with joy in his eyes to his grandchildren who graces him in unconditional affection. That spring of love that sits in his mind is so quick, it brushes by like a breeze in the wind. Those deep memories although wanted, what really grabs hold to his mind like a strangler is all his past misdeeds that haunt his dreams matching a presence in similarity to a deranged murderer that hang over his psyche in a cloud of gloomy karma awaiting to strike a fatal bite as an east indian cobra. The deeds of wrong he's committed proudly out of his own wicked in nature character. He's cheated on his wife numerously, abused liquor and drugs daily. With numerous of more treachery of the damned with his name written all over it. The man just lies there in his pain not knowing when and what time the reaper of death will escort him into the probable direction of eternal damnation for his hidden sins.

The paramedics have just made it to the emergency ward and placed the sickly man inside a room for the time being. Exchanging him from the gurney to the room bed. A nurse then insists on the son and wife to await outside until further notice from the doctor. They grow angry especially the son screaming and shouting at her that the man is his father and other intimidating phrases.
" Do you know who he is ?."
" Do you know who I am ? "

The nurse continues with her persuading the family. While the doctors circle the man checking his conditions, doing all they can to keep him breathing. The wife and son finally complies and exit from the room after security becomes involved to the nurse's aid. The son yells inside the room as he's warded off at the top of his lungs. " FIGHT IT". The security slams the room door shut behind him with strength so much so that you could feel it in every other room on the floor. Leaving the body of doctors behind him to take action on repairing the health of the man in a mode of physical declining.

1.CHAPTER

The man stuck on the bed of wheels with his eyes drifting off and on, his white skin damped in a bath of sweat, and his state of health looking to be pure pain from the opposite of reflection, is a very important man. A being who holds his place on the pulse of society. ERNEST MILES ST.CLAIR hold his physical place as a councilman for the American government and has served his place for over thirty years. As a lawgiver he's at the forefront of some of this country's most monumental law creations that were concerted for beneficial reasoning that were said to assert this country, and make it the more powerful nation that is. But that regular proverb has anything but honesty that does right to the statement. ERNEST in alignment with the circle of his fellow compatriots has done nothing with his prestigious position but made the life of the prosper more of affluent and opulent. While those who are on the side of the worlds neglect become farther and deeper into destitution and depletion. And upon their struggle of turmoil gains a better concealment from this country along a more enhanced disregard for those of less fortunate.

ONE HOUR BEFORE...

ERNEST and DAISY rest themselves peacefully seated at round table covered in gold cloth where the plates are china white and the utensils are shimmering silver glaring the ceiling beam off of them. The distinguishing restaurant that they incline themselves in for the evening holds a medium amount of guest. Faces that are no different than in expression from ERNEST or DAISY. They're the faces of the elite, those who strangle wealth in the city from politicians, liberals, republicans, democrats, analysts and all.

The mature tight couple ponder on conversation while awaiting the arrival of their son ALEX who's suppose to accompany them any minute with his newly married wife CLARISSA who's just arrived back from their honeymoon in ITALY. ERNEST who's feeling a little bit under the weather discusses to DAISY how much he cannot wait until he get back home to bed after being sprung with his rapid ill symptoms. That arrive too sudden at the occasion.

- You think it's a summer flu.

- I don't know but whatever it is, it has me so deep in the rim of its ass. I smell what it had lunch.

- Ernest please remember where we are. You wanna go now, we can postpone with ALEX. He'll understand.

- No... I don't want him worrying, besides he'll just make it probably worst with bringing that funny looking half Jew bitch by. Denigrating the threshold to our new home.

- ERNEST... Watch your mouth.

-What !!! DAISY you and I both know that whore doesn't care about our son. She saw a free trip and crawled aboard. And he going to see as time move forward too.

- Well I happen to like CLARISSA. She's very beautiful...but giving this was the depression time and we were in Nazi occupied space. And she was fibbing great on who she was. I'd spill on her to Hitler personally. With no regret in my heart as she'd escorted in the gas chamber at Dachau.

- That's what I thought...

- Here they are.

ALEX and his wife CLARISSA have been showed to their direction by the restaurant's greeter. On they're feet to embrace them both with hugs, kisses, and smiles is DAISY with some mediocre assistance from ERNEST with his wounded demeanor.

- I see things have became diverse here with the colored-jig waiters.

ALEX alludes after the departure of the greeter. ERNEST and DAISY cackles along with ALEX at his bigoted joke.

- The son's humor don't fall far the father's tree.

DAISY exhorts out loud. ERNEST laughs turns into harsh coughs that can't go unforeseen without care.

- You don't look to good, Dad. You alright !

- I'm fine son, just a little cold. Can't be any worst than these pieces of shit I have to deal with up at the damn snow cone looking capital. Screaming for this and that, the poor deserves this, while the rich has that. Nothing but integrating nonsense, I hear it so much now I might as well puke my fucking hearing out just to get away from it all. How was your two honeymoon ?

He asks.

- Unforgettable and beautiful. The view, our time, the air was oh my god. An unreal experience.

CLARISSA words while clutching her arm in excitement around Alex's arm embracing her happiness.

The waiter draws to the table armed with a smile and politeness appearing to be ready to take their orders of entrees and beverages for the evening. When he's done ERNEST excuses himself to the bathroom where he baths his face in cold water trying to relieve some the sickness feeling that hovers over him in distress. He gazes at his reflection in the restroom mirror poorly when he's refreshed, just before slipping his damped hands into his pocket. When he takes his hand out, he's palming a bag no bigger than a piece of small paper that's a sealable plastic covered in the color green. ERNEST pops the bag open quickly, slides some of the white contents it contains onto the even of his index finger, then snorts away. Sharing the attending treatment to both of his nostrils at once. When his high touches him instantly his eyes shoot back then jolt upward as he sniffs his nose a few dozen times. Clinched with his euphoria.

Once he's back at the table, ALEX greets him with comfort in concern" You alright dad ?". With his head lowered so no one can see the red in his eyes while under the influence of the powder. He replies back with a few more dozens of sniffs from his nose " Everything will be alright, once I get some rest maybe." DAISY soothes his back once he's in his seat with her hand and whispers that she ordered his usual craving, the roast beef for him. ERNEST tries his best to proceed on from his own irritant plight and asks CLARISSA how's her parents and their chain of business, a small talk for mind clearing. Responding in cheer, as she goes on informing that business is the same. Incomes the waiter chugging a crafty silver wheel cart to their table served on the deck with dishes that are devoted to everyone's wanting appetite. No one ceases in listening to CLARISSA carry on in dialogue while the server places down each platter directly in front of it rightful recipient. ERNEST still zoomed off the elevated ecstasy takes a sip of his water while eyeing CLARISSA mouth as she speaks and the food placement. He senses a unusual titillation and from his movement he must have never experienced it before. He rubs his right arm as if its not there firmly, his heart begins to race so agile he can hear it beating like a knock at a door, his eyes roll back into his head almost like his blood is being flushed from every pore of his body. Looking on is ALEX, he shouts at his dad in worriment "Dad ... Dad are you ok?". ERNEST is unresponsive to his question and tries to raise himself from his seat and as he does he falls back into it, clutching his arm as he tumbles backwards on the floor while everyone looks on with his face drenched in panic and pouring sweat. DAISY yells out and kneels to his aid opening his shirt and yelling his name. ALEX at the top of his lungs with CLARISSA behind him " SOMEONE CALL THE AMBULANCE... NOW MY DAD NEEDS HELP".

HOURS LATER --

With ERNEST in a deep state of unconsciousness as he's placed inside the comforts of a room under the number address 404 cardiac ward. Suspended in his snooze of rest with tubes inching out several places from his mouth and both arms. At his bedside propped on a shelf with more technical equipment beginning the foundation of the hoses that aid his health at the moment. What he'd undergone at the restaurant earlier was a severe stage heart attack.

A series of test are administered by a team of the hospital's most supreme doctors. They round up their conclusion on ERNEST'S health and deliver his results to his family. The news brings discomforting heartfelt, DAISY makes her screams known outwardly. There's nothing for Alex to do but to cradle his mother holding back tears of his own. Troubled with a glimpse of inner agony covers on his face.

In 404, ERNEST stunningly to all that look over him from family and physicians awakens back into revival. Poorly in state with his face coated in sluggish, appearing hard to not even make a move in fright of coming into interaction with pain. Lastly his eyes seep open in a bare crack, the first of what he sees is DAISY caressing his lifeless hand with her face displaying the soreness of the situation burdening her heart for her beloved partner unstable in his condition. ALEX stands close by behind her in support. DAISY pleads in a mirage of " shhh's" for ERNEST to remain quiet as possible until he can generate enough strength to overcome his sickly condition. If its possible at this point. Things reside indecisive in alignment with his health.

Time moves on through the hours as they cling to his side. Loyal in his time of need, DAISY in a chair closest to ERNEST side lays peacefully asleep unheard of cradling his hand like he's going somewhere. Managing enough will to raise both of their hands in place together, ERNEST does and pecks a kiss over her hand in intimate affection. From his opposite side is ALEX who makes himself known.

- How you doing pop ?

He words softly.

ERNEST then grabs his hand firmly before announcing with as much strength he can muster to voice.

-Shitty.

He then signals with his other finger for him to come closer. ALEX drags a chair next to the bed and gathers himself as close as possible next to his father.

- What did they tell your mother so far ?

ERNEST asks anxiously.

- From all the tests they've ran haven't been good pop. Your kidneys failing, you aren't responding well to the medicine they have you on, and they're calling your accident at dinner a coronary artery spasm.

He clarifies.

- A heart attack.

ERNEST affirms in worries.

- The doctors say its a godsend you reached the hospital when you did, they said the grams of cocaine in your system had a inch to kill you. Even after they didn't have plans to expect your awakening. None of us did. Mom had Father Ross to come by and say a prayer over you a couple hours back. She requested to him to make it two ... one for your soul and the other to cleanse you from your demons. It seems his trip wasn't for nothing.

ERNEST sheds a tear from his face in disbelief to all that has happened and how miraculous he is that he's still with life. He asks ALEX another question in appearance for desperation to know.

- What they got fixed up for me in regards to my condition decline.

- I passed on twenty grand for the lead specialists Doctor Auburn to place your name ahead of the donors list. He said between tomorrow and after he'd know something for sure. But I'm still waiting...

He explains.

- No, no you tell him keep that money and keep me on as much hard meds that they can find to suppress the pain for the time being. I need you to do something for me also.

He commands in his stable weakness.

- Anything... What ?

ALEX committed to his father's demand.

- First... I need my wallet, they didn't take it did they.

He asks.

Racing to the corner where there's a cupboard. ALEX opens it and pulls out his pants then raids the pants for his wallet as asked of him.

- I got it here.

He declares.

ERNEST instructs him precisely as he pursues through his personals to find a significant card that he explained was in a ordinary penmanship under a name and number. The scribbled words laid face on a average white blank card that from ERNEST recollection has to be stored not very distant. ALEX stumbles over the card at first then his mind triggers the description told to him by his father and within seconds there it is in front of him. He snatches it out of the fold then holds it in his fingers. In bold letters the fronting of the card in red ink reads the name " MOISSON SERVICES". ALEX doesn't hesitate after his discovery by being audible with the name.

- I want you call that number and ask to speak directly to a MR. MOSS. You tell whoever on the other side that your speaking from a second party of ERNEST ST.CLAIR and its urgent. They're well familiar with me so don't worry.

Enlighten with the design of orders. In no time he heads off like a messenger of proficiency embarking on fulfilling his new parental itinerary mission. Downstairs on the outside of the hospital near a vacant bus stop he makes a phone call using the number off the card to the mystery organization of "MOISSON SERVICES". A few punches to the numeral pad, the tone he hears hums then pauses between seconds. On the third wait there's a glitch that he hears from the ringing signal. Then there's a immediate scratchy female voice that can curdle a listener instantaneously, the lady must be mature in age. Once the freakishly creep accent sets over, she welcomes the conversation with a greeting.

- Good evening MOISSON SERVICES, this is MARGARET how can I help you ?

- I'm fine I'm wondering if it isn't too much for me have the liberty to speak with a Mr. Moss.

- May I ask who's speaking and what is this discussion with Mr. Moss is pertaining to late this evening.

She replies confidently in her cryptic tongue.

- My outreach to him is of urgency and desperation. I'm on this line speaking directly from a second party of a ERNEST ST. CLAIR...

He cries in patience.

- Long Pause-

- Say no more, on the behalf of MR. ST.CLAIR, wait one minute so I can transfer you over.

It's only a handful of seconds before the vacant transfer line holds another voice, this time a male and from his reaction it sound as if he was in a hurry.

- Hello this is MOSS and who do I owe this hankering at my precious time too.

- It's for my father ERNEST ST. CLAIR. I was told strictly from him to deal with you and only you for the desire that is way beyond my knowing.

Real quick he tells.

- Yea I know ERNEST, a real friend in need. His status is it life or death?

- It's DEATH which is why I explain so urgent. Look Mr. Moss this is serious and I don't know how much time he has left.

- Ok, I'm going to transfer you back over to the woman and she's going to provide a address for you. Tomorrow at three you be at that address and we'll get everything squared away for you and your father in no time. It's more than a favor to help a friend such as ERNEST.

The receptionist MARGARET passes on to ALEX the address . The next day at the nose of three o'clock there here is at the residence he was provided. The outfit of the quarters was in a common landmark on a bit of the outskirts of the city. There was breathing space but not vacant, peeping out the window of his vehicle. ALEX looks again at the address he jotted down the night before to make sure his directions was intact. The place rested in a old constructed brown store front that without recognition it could be almost labeled abandoned. He's thrown off a little when he sees that the residence isn't bearing any name entitlement over the doorway for customer attraction. Not a very wise marketing goal he thinks to himself before making his entrance inside anyways.

Upon ALEX entrance, he sets his eyes on dozens of shelves that stretched at least well over seven feet tall, they were wooden and sort of real antique almost. Filled with rows and rows of books that look to be from the 1800's. The floor was carpeted in a color of dirt that had been collected over time, the walls the same as well tribute black and white printed posters with pictures of old conservative white men who seemed as if they we're origin moguls of lawmaking in the American country. Some of their names were visible below their images held in honor like Benjamin Rush, Samuel Cartwright, Dr. Walter F. Jones, Dr. Robert G. Jennings, and Dr. Charles White. Once the astonishment blows over from the prehistoric book haven. ALEX finds his way to a counter where placed behind is a woman who widens a smile at him with very intimidating eyes of scare within them. She welcomes him.

- Hello, can I interest you in any of our catalogue of reading material today, young man.

The sound of her jolting voice is extremely familiar.

- My name is ALEX, I believe we spoke on the phone last night through MR. MOSS. MARGARET is it ?

Her eyes brighten even more in her recollection.

- Yes we did... And it's perfect your right on your time.

Peeping her direction toward a clock that hung over ALEX head over by the entrance.

- Give me one minute.

She gets on the phone and cues MR. MOSS that ALEX has arrived for their appointment just as he expected. When the phone goes down she follows with.

- You can come with me this way.

As escort she paces him through a back room that is a gateway to pitch black silence, there's a stair path not too far down, then another passing through a secured locked door. Where they enter finally its like a whole different environment opening. A complete contrast to the secluded library he prior had a acquaintance with before. The new space they were in now had a body of what looks to be crew members all around congregating and working. ALEX is in all as he views females holding calls at desks, men shuffling files in their offices, people typing away at computer screens, drinking coffee, joking, security guards in full blown uniforms checking the perimeters on their monitors, average joes from old and frail to young and vibrant all confined to a small area awaiting for numbers they have to be called for in comparison to a local clinic. You could hear employees at a nearby register counter speaking on a public announcer in a formal tone calling for the next visitor by number and additional the concern responsible for their appointment. With the rotation identical to being attended in a motor vehicle headquarters.

" Number 21E/HEART you now will be seen at Office four. 22F/LUNG your at Office 1."

After the trip of fascination MARGARET brings ALEX to a door at the end of a very small hall away from the busy rush, they stop in front of and in courtesy she knocks twice with a voice on the other side that can be heard mouthing " YES ". Handling the knob for the open MARGARET enters first with ALEX behind.

There at a wall standing with his back to the front appearing to be reading something that sits in his hands is MR. MOSS. On his feet in front of a colossal size mural of a man very similar to the posters that sat on the walls by the shelves of books when in introduction to the building. The view out looked almost over his complete back wall, absorbing ALEX'S attention right of way.

- Here he is MR. MOSS, ALEX ST. CLAIR.

Reaching his hand out for a gentleman shake brandishing a smile that seemed to harbor sinister deceptions. ALEX returns the expression properly gaining a up and down of MR. MOSS from his hairless head, tight face, and cold blue eyes. After MARGARET leaves the both of them alone to discuss the fixing of his ordeal.

- Don't worry I'll try make this as fast as possible at the sake of your father, so don't worry that inner anticipation and rest yourself. Please.

- Thank you !

Suggesting ALEX takes access to one of the chair's in front of his desk. And he does while still having focuses on the big picture that can yank the average persons focal point away from them in a blink of an eye. MR. MOSS grieves his empathy in a show of respect to ALEX. Reminding him how much of a friend his father is to him which is why he has no problem helping a friend like his dad when times like this strike. MR. MOSS moves into business as usual and reveals a few pieces of documents that he wish to lend ALEX'S signature to. It beholds a few small papers with tiny words of discretion which he doesn't bother to carefully read but skim over with his eyes. There then is a surrender of a check enclosing a payment of fifty thousand dollars with an additional promise between both parties that another transaction of fifty thousand be provided at haste time. Once his father's care grows to elevation. It hasn't even been more than ten minutes as they are in the midst to conclude their meeting when something nerves ALEX that he can't help to ask who is the mural of the man that sits behind him in a appearing righteous commemoration. MR. MOSS who acts as if that mentioning never gets old to him as he twists his chair around in observation to the boy's question. His clarification is nothing but pure adoration as he spills it clean to ALEX. Lifting himself from his chair and planting both feet directly in front of the heavy weight figure grasping in its essence like it releases energy of triumph or nobleness. Although ALEX gives off a completely different reaction staring at the pressuring portrait confined to his chair in gaping misery.

- Please... I get that question asked to me all the time. So much so I'm starting to think about having surgery with it being tattooed in my psyche. Don't worry that was a joke...that man there above was significant in surgery and even more advancing in the works of gynecology. He was a great, great, great, great, great uncle of mines Dr. James Marion Sims, a pioneer physician that opened the door to the modern technology we have today. He was held to esteem power even here in the present with his name and image living on in statues of honor and to others that power trickled down to him in relation to insanity and scrutiny. Doesn't take much thought on to which side of difference I'm loyal too as bold as you can see.

- I have to say it is intimidating on sight...

- I agree...well it seems we're just about finished here.

- Are we ? I mean I only been here for not even closing ten minutes. This is routine.

- I'm afraid so... But there is just one more important thing I'll need from you before you step outside that very door from which you came.

Vanishing the comfort of his ego and elevating it into seriousness.

- And what is that ?

He leans over the desk and reaches his hand out with his sinister looking grin that must be apart of his temperament. ALEX mimics the same and they shake hands as MR. MOSS smiles from ear to ear as everything is finalize...

2.CHAPTER

In a tin grey colored steel chair a male figure sits down and gently steps his size eleven feet into a pair of fairly new Adidas sneakers each individually before lacing them tightly. When finished there's a routine of hamstring stretches on a floor being administered each with vocal counts to the number twenty, large pumping veins pierce through the brown skin of the lengthy legs covered in brawn and robust. He continues working his hip and outer thigh, inner thigh, on his feet standing thigh stretch, arm and back, and lastly shoulder and back exercises. Like its all a habitual workout he's done over and over countless days and nights.

Stepping onto a hardwood floor with his steps of assured manhood echoing a gymnasium like a person shouting off a canyon. He grabs a orange basketball scripted with the words Spaulding in cursive text on the front of it. Then proceeds into a art of dribbling formations that are architected with pure skill and destiny. Starting off very slow with a one-two; with bringing the ball through one of his legs and then back out. Then a three-four which consists to bringing the ball between his left leg and then his right. In no time he stands just passing the ball through his legs while adjusting them in a automated switch in agility back and forth both way and ends to the court. In moments he demonstrates his moves on the court with defenders practicing in their greatest might to contest his ability of beauty as he all out crossovers his competitors in a style that has yet to be seen before the world on a global scale. Working his teammates in and out even in one point twirling the ball behind his back in maneuvers beating them one way and going another, some are even made silly with the confusion of his dribbling madness. Members confined to the bench view or bleachers seats shout out phrases in amazement to the man's repertoire while looking on.

" DO YOUR THING SHAWTY"

" SHOW EM SOMETHING"

" NBA HERE HE COME"

" MAGIC CAN'T FUCK WITH HIM"

" DOC CAN'T FUCK WITH HIM"

" LARRY THE WHITE BOY, YOU TRIPPIN"

In his many attempts rising to the occasion leaving his compatriots victims to his craft of basketball perfection. He then decides to begin in tossing up jump shots like free throws leaving the net caroling the sounds over and over again. SWOOSH... As he pulls up twenty feet from mid corner, SWOOSH... He pulls up twenty five feet top of the key, SWOOSH... Thirty feet near mid court... SWOOSH, many gazing nothing but the ball seeping through the net without luck or charm. Just simply pure natural divine artistry that has chosen him to flaunt through talent. Coming off his lunging three pointer display running full speed of flight towards the rim. Ahead of him standing under the hole is a teammate of his who's springing a ball up and down from his hands real attentive as he watches the man dashing at him in jolt. Once he gets closer he slings the ball in bounce from the hardwood floor as hard as he can with it ascending far up into the air. The man timing the ball, lifts himself into mid air over the hoop shooting inside the free throw territory as the ball graces into his right hand like a wizard and him slamming it in one-handed with aggression, for a unspeakable playground term entitled "alley-oop". The miniature circle of people inside the room go into a frenzy of captivation as a boisterous whistle noise overwhelms the atmosphere after his clutching stunt. When the man feet touches the floor from a show move he had just gave. Everything transitions into a real game being played in exhibition of the season and no longer the past tense tutorial he was previously trailblazing. The arena with the rows of seats that were empty before, now house a full capacity of seekers in pandemonium of cheers and celebration. Some even stand in bunches at every corner of the facilities exit spaces just to get a glimpse of this new sport sensation.

The man who just declared his ability of expertise in a commendable presentation, even though his mass build frame resembles a maturing athletic gladiator, his gargantuan feet size, standing a impressive height of six foot three and a half inches and growing. The man isn't a man not as yet, he is still a boy of the tender age of fourteen years old. His stature speaks but his minor face that sprouts a few pimples from his beginning stages of puberty say different especially with his high flying aerial moves. He doesn't even have facial hair lingering from up under his nose at the moment.

As the height of the game flows on in the rhythm of excitement with this kid's overbearing defying moves of impeccability that strongholds the floor in his palms. Entering a side door of the gymnasium from the outside halls of the school immediately confronted with the crowd of teenagers that parade the area as if they own it. Is a OLDER GENTLEMEN dressed business formal head to toe. He wears huge glasses that shield his eyes and a beige raincoat, standing tall enough to peep over the crowd of misfits and into the floor where the game goes on. He hasn't even laid his eyes on every player yet but to a few kid's standing in front of them blurting out names of players that they know out of encouragement to remain a force in the competition. The OLDER GENTLEMEN stands and hears the two dialogue before he accosts into their conversation out of plain respect.

- Hey you two know these teams.

The man says real easy and non threatening. One of the teens breaks it down for him simple.

- See that team in the green who getting they ass beat, that's Aztec Academy. The dudes in orange who up by twenty on them that's the home school Wilson.

- Wilson's good ?

Surprised from the score difference also in curiosity to Wilson's potential as a team.

- They wasn't shit until this year when they lucked up on ROCKET coming here.

The other teen informs.

- ROCKET ?

In confusion to his last statement.

- Yea Robert Rocket, the only next dude in line to take this whole game by storm like Magic, once he get his feet in.

The two teens laugh while sharing a slap of hands for having identical opinions. Still curious to this player called ROCKET. The OLDER GENTLEMEN asks kindly for the teens if they could finger this up and coming superstar on the floor.

- He right there number thirty- three. Who you ?

The teen asks in deep curiosity after informing.

- He a fed....

Just before the OLDER GENTLEMEN counters the offensive question. Suddenly ROCKET gets the ball in his hands and blows by two defenders like a magician equipped with a round orange ball he and only he has the competence to navigate swiftly. In seconds after reaching the key he sails above in the air like a canary over Aztec's six foot eight center and slams it home single handedly. The whole room of people explode in applauses and cheers on their feet for ROCKET including the two teens and the OLDER GENTLEMEN looking on.

- I'm a scout for a local university.

Revealing a handy card of his with his name RONALD HART in bold letters from his jacket. The two kids laugh and point across the room on the other side of the gym where enclosed to the middle of crowd seated on the bleachers are four scouts already looking and some are even jotting down notes about ROCKET the sensation. One of the teens in the midst of his laughter spills out while chuckling.

- Hope you didn't think you'd be first in the rat race. That competition been out the door slim.

The OLD GENTLEMEN shoots back at the comical teens real clever.

- Maybe I wanted to check if the prize had accrued any value before the pistol fired.

As the game nears end to closure. The entire auditorium assembles as one counting down the last seconds of the game that ROCKET leading Wilson performed another shutout on their opponent at they're stomping home grounds once again. The two teens join in the countdown with it narrowing down FIVE, FOUR, THREE, TWO, ONE. The horn blows and the bleachers filled to the top with people, clear to the floor crowding the team and specifically the guy who put on a clinic in performance for the evening statistically with a outstanding 41pts, 6asts,

9rbs, and a remarkable 4 steals in addition. ROBERT ROCKET who's last capture thrusting the ball in the air with all his might as a mark for the end of the game, celebrates with exuberant cheerfulness. His face glares with smiles surrounded by the audience crowd and his teammates basking in the glory of victory.

When the two teens wonder in the pool of merriment, jumping up and down in glee. RONALD looks on remaining distant with a meager smile as he sees a few of the scouts shower ROCKET with introductions and handshakes in liking to his impressive execution for style of play. RONALD HART the old gentlemen share a few more seconds of staring at this rising basketball phenom. Then exits back outside the door into the hall as he came leaving the gymnasium in a roar of excitement.

The game is over and majority of the gym is empty despite the larger than life onlookers who commanded their occupancy once the game had ruled their attention minutes before. Some of the people continue to depart as the remaining of the team show themselves to the exit sign after leaving the locker rooms. The janitorial team begin the daily reconstruction repair of the school's assembly property from tonight's regular function and on the floor speaking before his farewell to a couple more scouts is ROCKET with his gym bag swung around his shoulder, his hands tightly gripped on the straps as a sign of nervousness. He leaves them in handshakes then out the exit door all by himself. Upon the nightfall in the parking lot he clowns with a few teammates momentarily and even is approached to sign a few mesmerized kids Wilson team shirts that are retail as souvenirs during the games, just before he leaves. The partings is in two different directions, some of his teammates walk or head off in vehicles one direction, while ROCKET goes in the other waving them goodbye in a distance.

Sprinting his way across the dark street with vehicles floating pass, he makes his way just in time to a bus that's in route to his home destination. After paying, he adjusts himself to a seat and rests himself in patience to his ending source.

Arriving to his destination he exits from the bus and proceeds to walk the rest of the way. Helping himself to a apple in hunger walking by in a quiet residential neighborhood filled on both opposite sides of the street with well constructed homes that are adjacent to their grassy green lawns and cozy homely driveways. Occasionally as he strolls ROCKET catches glimpses of these complimenting homes, but really he stays focus us on his march. With his hands in his pocket, stride in his step, and duffle bag mixed with school and basketball material dangling strapped to his shoulder like a seatbelt. Same as the vehicle phrase is hinted, slowly comes creeping beside of the young teenager in his journey home is a dark burgundy car, in it is a older gentlemen, he's RONALD the scout who held away at distance from the floor at the game. With his window cracked down that easily identifies his appearance perfectly. ROCKET stopped in his footing followed by his apple munching, bends down peeping in expectations to what the man wants.

- You look stupid so I'm a give you a head start to keep going up the street before I yank you out that car and close your head in the fuckin door.

Angrily he utters with his eyes locked dead on RONALD as if he's seriously capable of his threats.

- Woah easy I'm just a fan kid, I saw your game and you have talent.

RONALD responds.

- What ?

ROCKET asks.

- Tonight I saw you do things on that court that can take you very far in your future. I saw your numbers kid.

He says.

- I talk to enough scouts for tonight, and I heard enough promises. I am a person you know that right, we do have lives other than spinning a ball on our finger to your amusement.

The boy tells him. RONALD laughs real subtle.

- This isn't a harassment call.

RONALD says.

- What is this then ?

ROCKET cries.

- This is fan to player, the adorer to greatness. I'm RONALD HART.

Before ROCKET can even think to introduce himself even when his disdain is too visible. RONALD does it for him as a token of authentic admiration.

- And your ROBERT ROCKET. The number one basketball prospect in the state, a shoe in for MR. BASKETBALL, I've been reading about you since your playground tournament days at Goodman league since you were ten.

The conversation transitions into a different interaction oppose to the one before where ROCKET stood bending down peeping into the car. Instead now he's carefully walking while still talking to RONALD as he trails him at a slow pace in his car. The middle class homes in beauty begin to fade and they cross into a new territory that are plagued with winos walking around, rugged apartment fronts, and liquor store lights beaming bright into the gutter of disenfranchisement.

- What do you want ?

ROCKET asks.

- Why should I want something ?

RONALD presumes.

- Look stop running game man, I'm tired, you don't know the things that you know about a fourteen year old who can slam a ball into a hoop unless it was worth your time. And time is money...so say what you want ?

ROCKET demands.

- Alright kid you got me, I am a scout and all I want to do is help you... There are a lot vultures out there and they're all going to promise you so many things on your ride to the top, if they haven't already. And they might succeed because I see the charisma and bark in you not like the others but I still want to help you.

ROCKET stops in his pace again and stoops down outside his passenger window staring RONALD in the eyes another go around.

- How are you going to help me ?

He asks me.

At the end of his statement instantaneously a sound is heard. And it's RONALD unlocking all four of his car doors. A suggestion for ROCKET to enter.

- Get in and we can talk about it while I dropped you off on the way home. Ten minutes is all I ask for.

The two share a period mute in their speech. ROCKET looks at RONALD in the eye for the third time. Staring through all his clever rhetoric and schematic deceptions that is written over his face in black marker. RONALD serves a look of anxiousness to his decision. Still gaining a observation, suddenly a miscellaneous voice is shouted and heard that grabs both of their attention. " Ayy ROCKET " in seconds ROCKET eyes shoots to the opposite side of the street and RONALD follows. Across the street are a few younger dudes all standing before a storefront like a congregation. One of them in a cap shoved low on his head must know ROCKET as he continues calling. RONALD looks on in his own disappointing curiosity. " You good " the man says tending to the scene with it blatantly apparent that the vehicle must be bothering him. RONALD catches on to the subliminal street wording that's being emphasized and he turns the lock back on to his vehicle doors in worry. But ROCKET doesn't notice, he stares back at RONALD who's clear to the position of possible trouble he's in at the signal of the boy. Trembling and doubling his eyes to those across the street and ROCKET who's steady eyeing him and even smirks to his sudden fear. ROCKET

takes one more good look at the old man and daringly screams over "
HE LOOKING FOR SOME WORK". RONALD eyes brightened in fear
as the boy points across the street and incomes the mini mob of young
men, all bigger and much more older than ROCKET diving in the busy
street in pursuit to their rally point where the burgundy car stands.
RONALD clutches his hand on his steering wheel and shift gears to
drive with his feet flooring the gas pedal and speeds off from ROCKET
and their conversation in a carbon copy way to a drag racer out of his
suspiciousness. When the group makes to the other side they exchange
hand greets with ROCKET as he's laughing from the whole scenario as
RONALD boots up the street in velocity.

The next game at Wilson, ROCKET and his team of ordinaries team up
against a wrecking crew of hard boiled opponents from the rough section
of the south side of the city that also held honors in being undefeated.
The two went head to head in battle for a classic game fueled with
maturing testosterone competitiveness, both in seek for domination over
the other. ROCKET has his best game yet since the season opener
issuing a unheard of forty-nine points, snatching twelve boards, and
seven dishes. He not only withstood the overbearing showcase test the
rival team made accessible to him in the order of scratch and clawing but
he showed how resilient he could play at a level circled with that much
passion. He capped the game off with sinking two critical devastating
free throws to stake claim for the win as well as another performance to
be held special and told on and on giving this kid more mythical clout to
add on into his school wide legend.

After showering and heading as fast as he could to the bus stop on his
way home. He's stopped by his coach and another gentlemen who is
solidified by his coach as a friend. The man was a older white male in
his later sixties with white slick hair and bearing light tinted lenses in his
shades. Partnered with a jolly grin the man welcomes himself as an

assistant for a native NBA team. Then his coach informs during their conversation that this assistant was interesting in setting a date having him workout with a few of the players on the team only a gesture of friendliness to his superb gaming skills. But this proposition was only accessed if ROCKET was opened to the idea first. The boy grins just as the assistant did upon his first glance at him and concludes that he'll think on it while on his bus ride home. They are both understanding to his decision and before he's off on his path, he's offered a ride home but he insists on his own transportation approval. He leaves the two gentlemen in the gymnasium with a pair of handshakes and goodbyes as he's out the door with above syllables beaming red lights that spell out the words EXIT.

Gazing outside into a view of economic disproportion. ROCKET stares in a trance from his bus ride window at a completely opposite difference of economic exposure from two separate communities that awaits his eyes in watching. Without showing emotional reaction to the class inequality. The representation in one area shows growth flourishing with occupied model homes, equipped office buildings, playground hardtops with off white nettings that seems to be hardly used, along with trails of substantial eatery places in all cultures and fresh produce markets. While the other area circulates its composition shortly after in route uncovering a complete dissimilarity to the very first space. Revealing boarded homes in decay that collect dust and dirt over seasonal transitions, free clinics that specializes in abortion operations and vaccinations for diseases, dungeon buildings that are housed as schools, liquor fronts and cheap Chinese food carry-outs with numerous patrons of the underworld and addiction taking up space directly nearby.

Stepping onto the bus dropping her change into the fee machine and collecting herself a seat not too far from where ROCKET holds his gawk at a lack of balance in his reality. The girl rushes sorting through her purse as if something inside have lost its way from it. Sniffing her nose at tears shooting down her face, whimpering low but loud enough to grab ROCKET'S concentration from his original activity. When he notices the girl's sad emotional state, he looks on for a moment in desperation and then aids her in support by fixing himself to an open seat that is directly by her.

-Excuse me I don't mean to bother you, but are you going to be ok.

The girl is steady on with her crying. Her cheeks are blushed with moisture from the excessive wiping away she does with her hands. She insists on shifting through her purse of things in total disregard to his concern. So ROCKET giving the perception that his sense of care is a annoyance to her. He raises from the seat to leave her to her lonesome. As he stands in attempt to walk away she grabs his pants tightly with a firm grip, looks him in the eye and apologizes for her manner of rudeness.

- I'm sorry ... Please excuse me I didn't mean that its just my feelings are really fucked up and I shouldn't take it out on you especially when your the only person that's showed this bit of niceness to me all day.

He raises back down into the seat giving his plain attention to this girl who's beauty hadn't became a priority to him until this very moment of notice. She was a light red girl with lips that were full and well fitted for her, and wore her hair real short in small curls that appeared to be roughed up one side more than the other. While informing her to who he is, ROCKET extends his hand out to greet her respectfully as a gentlemen.

- I'm Robert...

She's receiving to his natural gesture of introduction.

- I'm Diane. I actually just moved here from Illinois.

- Yea I thought you sounded different, you look like it too.
Not in a bad way though.

He tells her.

- Thank you... this is my first week here and it already seems like I'm getting tested by everybody, by my house and at school. Why can't everybody be as easy and cool like you.

She hints.

Frustrated she is as she pours her heart out in distress.

- I don't know...what school you go to ?

- Aztec...everyone there even the teachers calls it " Tec". Have you heard of it ?

She asks.

- Yea I know "Tec" my team just beat there's last week. I feel for you at that school, you in DA LAND...

He says.

Not comprehending the term and phrase in hinting too.

- Please don't remind me they have that word spray painted on a wall across from my locker. I just got into it with one of the girls who belong to their crew I think. I just finished from being in a fight with them. They ended up jumping me and I think one of them must've swipe my purse while I was down and stole my money. I had to use change to get on the bus. That's why I didn't speak to you before.

She explains.

- It's cool trust me I understand I had run ins with them all the time.

- How'd you deal with it.

- Just hold yours is all I can tell you, they're going to try you because you still new. You being cute don't help either. They'll leave you alone eventually once they feel like you stood your ground.

He refers to.

The two parlay their conversation between each other for the duration of the bus commute. Before her stop arrives DIANE grows a little weary before her exit off, ROCKET notices. Out with her inner anxiety she asks him if he would be inclined to walk her home. Luckily for her his residence is no more than six blocks down from his place of stay, so he agrees without hesitation. Her stop comes, she nudges the rope bell a couple times before stepping off the bus.

Traveling easy with DIANE'S building not too far away. The two breezes on into more conversation. DIANE becomes more interested in ROCKET painstakingly about his size and physical structure that assuming it must reflect to some athleticism. It isn't forthright in her dialogue but she does hints to it looking at him over and over like he's a giant. Finally catching on he asks her.

- What ? Why you keep looking at me like that.

(Chucking)

- Nothing I just can't get over how big and tall you are. You look like you can play every sport there is, I bet you do ?

She chuckles also to her assumption in compliments.

- No... I started out playing just football until one day about four or five years ago and I'll never forget. I was watching this basketball game between the spurs and rockets. And I saw these two dudes going at each other, putting on a show. It was David Thompson and George Gervin, Skywalker versus Iceman in a showdown for the last game of the regular season, until then I never even paid basketball any mind with being so consumed with football. But watching those two and how easily they could put the ball in the hoop did something to me, when the horn blew Ice had about sixty three, D.T had maybe seventy three. Ever since then and that game every time I'm on the court I imitate both of those players in that exact game over and over again.

- Wow ! That's nice, that's kind of like me and academics. Any schools after your talent yet.

She asks.

- Man its so many I can barely keep up with them. They all come to my games, staring at me like I'm some piece of meat. Asking me all these questions, old white men in my face smiling and laughing wanting to befriend me, my coach in shenanigans with them. You know last week a scout had to nerve to actually try and follow me home, around here.

- Really ? What you do ?

ROCKET goes over the story to her as they enter the doors of her building, the main door has to be unsecured with a key. The old and worn dwelling stood about three floors up. Ascending slowly up the stairs with DIANE leading the way, following on at him staying close to every word and detail he says. She leads him to a room at the end of a hall upon his climax of the story where they both share laughs with DIANE sending flirtatious signals with her eyes at ROCKET now that he has fulfilled a request that she had wished for.

Standing before the door to her home. Locked at sight of each other, face to face. The moment for their separate ways arrives unhappily at this time.

- So I probably see you on the bus tomorrow.

He tells her.

- I hope so. Can I give you something just in case I don't because I really am thankful to you helping me today. You didn't have to...

She says.

- But I did and don't trip its cool.

- Ok...

Gleaming a smile at him, they stand there for seconds that seems to be hours before DIANE pursues to lean in at ROCKET, puckering her lips out towards him. ROCKET in the moment just as her, exchanges the motion and too lunges in for what her gift to him must be a kiss. Just as they are about to make it, DIANE divests and snaps herself out of the mood simply due to embarrassment.

- Oh my god, I'm so sorry. I'm a little embarrassed. I - I- I never done...

(Chuckling)

- ...this before, yea I can tell.

Completing her final statement that she stutters out nervousness.

DIANE submits one final request at ROCKET in hopes he can agree once again for her.

- With this being my first time, you think maybe you could close your eyes for me this one time. I'm so nervous I can feel my heart popping in my chest.

He doesn't say anything but reacts to her offer pleasantly by closing his eyes with certainty and even going further as to cover them with his hand for her purposes only.

Lastly they agree to countdown from three before their peck in bliss. As they go on, temporarily blinded ROCKET counts on naturally like the agreement.

THREE... TWO... ONE.

After he reaches one and nothing happens he assumes she must've grew scared again.

- Don't tell me with my eyes closed you still a little punk...

Until he hears a odd noise that resembles the expansion of paper or some sort.

- What's that ?

When ROCKET lifts his hand from his face and opens his eyes. Standing in front of him no different than before is DIANE only this time she's holding a torn piece of duct tape that she shoves over his mouth instantly with force covering any words that escapes from his voice. Behind him on cue the door of her suspected home nearly flies off the hinges as it opened by a huge framed man who snatches the young boy into his possession from behind with a single arm thrust around his neck. Feeling the overbearing pressure of his massive bicep clinching his throat, ROCKET screaming what looks as plentiful shouts that cant be made out in speech from the tape bound over his lips and his eyes bulging in fear. While panicking is then tugged inside the room like a doll by the colossal man with the durable strength of lumberjack. DIANE acting to the evident plan on instinct slams the door close directly after and the eerie rattle from the door being along with the terror tension in the air from the moment is the only noise that is heard throughout the vacant bare hall. Curdling commotion thumping around inside the apartment, sounds of stiff movement bouncing off the walls in a heavy tussle. There's cries out "HELP... HELP... SOMEBODY HELP" at the top of ROCKET'S lungs that can be heard through distortion. But unfortunately his pleas and screams for rescue won't be useful in his plight of wrenching shock. The weeping is heard once more deepened in agony, behind another swarm of force rattling. Then like a snap of a finger a split between minutes then and now. A gunshot rings out. His screams aren't there anymore...its gone.

3.CHAPTER

A symphony of melodic rock music waves its vibe from a residential home with an exterior look matching to distinguish. Outside of the attracting homestead where the combination of hippie and soul of the seventies tunes are being harmonized followed with sounds of an assembly going on. There's a young girl and boy nearby in the yard chasing each other around in a mood of minor fun carrying huge balloons enjoyed by their trinkets of celebration. The pair of youths then decide to take their outer exploration inside the house invading in sprint pass the screen door where there's a body of individuals consumed to the bass of loud music that's being played as some casual dance, talk between each other with pleasing smiles, and adoring laughs that fill the room. Others indulge themselves to food in the kitchen or the selective bar with rows bearing assorted exotic categorized wines and liquor. The place is littered with confetti on the floors, enormous balloons like the children paraded around with, and a huge banner positioned inside the living space where everyone seems to be placed texting the words " WELCOME HOME" in gigantic letters for everyone to lay eyes on.

The two youngsters continuing on in the party with their dashing and racing bring themselves to a halt when the boy is swipe into the arms of his mother CLARISSA, who employs them both to slow down their pace for safety.

- You two pump your brakes while your in this house, please...

Neighboring them in adjacent to the kitchen spot is an older couple holding themselves to the music boogie in a awkward sense of rhythmic movement that seems to be relative to them. The woman is DAISY grinning her teeth away in delight, serenading her way with the near full recovery from recent surgery is ERNEST. Now that he's gaining rehabilitation and no longer confined to a medic bed. From his looks and active spirit that he displays, his past health troubles that could of very assured him into fatality are now steps behind him currently. Its been a year since he's been home while recuperating in the hospital after having his organs replaced due to his previous ones closing in on stages to failure. The doctors advised that he stay admitted for tests on his bodily actions. Everything grew into the clear and before he knew he was finally released with a normal, stable, healthy condition. Once the good news was verified by ERNEST to his wife DAISY about his leave. She conjured up a unforgettable "WELCOME HOME" party on his behalf while inviting a list of good friends.

In the middle of the celebration breathing excitement into the air for everyone. A high volume pitch ring from the kitchen phone is heard. DAISY eases away to answer insisting for ERNEST to not worry and maintain his joy. The call is from ALEX who for some reason hasn't made his way in attendance to the tribute event for his father's homecoming as of yet. He clarifies to his mother upon the phone call his reasoning.

- Things have been going on for hours Alex, where are you ? Your father's expecting you?

Real uptight in her tone is DAISY.

- I know, I know I'm just deep into papers at work and most of these files have to be finished by next week in my department. What about Clarissa is she there yet ?

- She's right here with Thomas. The both of us were concerned a little.

DAISY transfers the phone over to CLARISSA who's looking on. ALEX early informed by his mother of her anxiety of his yet to be seen arrival. Quickly he summons an excuse to deliver her once she gains retrieval of the phone. In a bit of reluctance to his messaging CLARISSA consumes the very same response as DAISY from ALEX. He passes on that he'll be there later before anything ends. He then asks as a favor from his wife to have him speak with his father ERNEST who's living himself up on the dance floor. She agrees with a fuss and then has ERNEST to come over in his mood of comfort.

- Heeey son ! I've been looking all over for you, everybody here's and waiting for you.

ERNEST says in cheer screaming almost over the loud music.

- I'm finishing up things now pop, and I'm on my way to you. Never mind the party, how are you feeling ? The doctor said you should take it easy and still rehabilitate.

- I'm fine son, I never felt this good since I was forward on my school team. I was worst than dog shit but right now the way I'm feeling I can score a hundred points on any of those spooks in the NBA.

Alex chuckles in humor real shy.

- Since the mood is there when I get there we'll play a pickup game like old times. I'll be Rick Barry and you can be "Pistol Pete". Deal.

- Deal but the way I'm feeling I'm telling you son is invincible or untouched. I feel like that boy from Michigan State. What's his name Wizard Johnson.

ALEX corrects him.

- Dad its Magic Johnson.

- Yea him or that other one " Ice Cream" or " Ice Cold" .

- You mean George Gervin the "Ice Man".

- You got it, I'll see you once you get here.

- Ok pop.

When the phone call ends ALEX despite his allegations that he screamed to his mother, father, and wife that confined him to his duties at work. Found himself not in a place abiding task committals but more of a space seeking the fulfillment of lust.

For the past month ALEX has been lingering his obsessive passion with another women. Roaming the cities countless hotels establishments. Clinching both of their extreme appetites for raunchy non committed sex.
Seated at the side edge of the plushy, pampered bed matched for a rest stay complimentary to a couple of king and queen royalty closest to the dresser is ALEX slowly in thought placing the phone back on to its base. The look on his face shows his contempt to the lies he's just told to the people he's cared the most for in his world. Behind him cuddled in pillows and the finest white sheets from herself in relaxation covered in nothing but her exuberantly attractive lingerie that molds to her womanly figure like clay. Inching closer to him and his haunting

consciousness slowly caressing his ear with her ample thin lips is BELLE. As she tries in releasing him from his internal restrictions hoping to rejuvenate him to a mood of sensual night cap. Whispering on while in his ear.

- It's ok... I only need thirty minutes.

The words of her sexual easing comfort is all ALEX needs to here from luring utterance that BELLE mutters before they both are tussling through the sheets in a frenzy of rebellious delight. When the two succession in gaining each orgasmic ultimate's, they call it a night as ALEX drops BELLE off in front her door step with a mention as she leaves from his car that he'd talk to her tomorrow.

Infatuated with his own favors, and time now setting upon the light of the moon. It's an expected regret now that ALEX has dodged his father's welcoming home ceremony with promises that he would show. He knows that his broken pledges to his parents would be analyzed harshly though are bearable if they were to be in comparison to his true troubles in frustration. The most deep in his hidden mind closets is the brutal backlash he'll be subjected to by his wife not only from the assurance he gave her while on the phone, his over delayed return, but even more importantly than all the others is her growing instinctual figure of his suspecting fidelity. That's beginning to enhance larger and larger with his actions and unmet promises she notices. From the time ALEX steps inside his home well into he shuts his eyes he finds himself in a mild tempered game involving questions and answers from CLARISSA. With him putting up a cloak defense to deceive his real affection that supports her hunch of him being not loyal within the boundaries of their vows they've made together.

ERNEST has retired for the night after the day's explosion in alleviation catering to his defying recovery that led way to his warm return. Now that all his guest and friends have departed and are gone, the music is indefinite mute. DAISY lying next to him subdued to her dream state. There he is propped under the warm blankets that he grapples in his hands as he eyeballs upward into the darkness in his own mind state that resembles to be mystifying wide in his open vigilance. Almost as he cannot join himself with sleep, although he wants too.

Finally he jolts up from the covers soundless in the behalf of his wife as she rests peacefully. He preps himself in gym shorts, sneakers he wears when he cuts the grass, and a old worn academy shirt from his rookie days. Then cuffs a basketball from the garage. In the late hours of the night he walks a few blocks down to the local gym that circulates to the open prestigious district for twenty-four hours. Face to face in a open court that's plagued in desertion from any soul accept himself, he takes a few dribbles with the ball and begins to friendly toss up some jump shots in a way of a routine workout. He misses a few at first but when he settles himself and the only thing he can hear is his heart fueled with power. Beating in a rhythm of natural consciousness of a life, things click on like a light switch for him and before you know he's sinking every shot once his knees spring, and his feet elevate forces the ball to catch goal pass the steady metal rim through the soft netting. With his adrenaline running and pumping its way all through his veins and body, after setting dozens of shots mid to far range. Something in him possess the courage and the beyond ability as a middle age man who not more than a couple days earlier was helplessly detained to a automatic bed and to now hoisting from the squeaky noise clear floor floating the ball layup style into the hoop. Almost similar to perfection of well known playground ball move called the "Finger Roll". A gameplay tactic manifested by George Gervin, installed into his lift off repertoire to ward off any statue players from rejecting his shot.

The maneuver he did on his own is enough to send ERNEST back into the hospital. Once both of his feet are back on the floor like they'd always been for the rest of his life. Shocked to what just unfolded he can't believe what he has just done. First observing his legs, feet, hands, the ball, and turning face to the rim where he's done this at. It's thin edge to a dream for him even without him dreaming.

Strangely enough for him the next day. Still placed on leave from his job, DAISY awakes him for breakfast as she races out the door before coming into contact with her tardiness. She screams from downstairs that she's left his dawn meal on the dining room table with extra's still on the stove if wanted. ERNEST adventures down with his stomach craving in appetite when he's ready. What he sees according to his wife as she sped out the door mentioned it was his favorite. Isn't anything satisfactory to his craving expectations apparently. There on the table is a off brand of corn flakes with a glass filled to the neck of orange juice, and a bowl with a half split grapefruit. ERNEST with a expression of displeased tosses the grapefruit into the trash and the bowl of corn flakes meets it end to the garbage disposal even before they could moisten in flavor to the milk. The stock in the cabinets are just as worst.

He takes a trip to the grocery store wandering pass aisles he hasn't ever favor until now what with DAISY doing all the shopping regularly. Exploring aisles that hold ranges and ranges of any humans desire selection to cereal with mind rattling names apparently endorsed for children. Flavors, and attractive box front schemes like: Sugar pops, Kaboom, Cap'n Crunch, Alpha-Bits, Fruit Brute, Moonstones, Crunchy loggs, Pink Panther Flakes, Sugar Smacks, Cocoa Crispies. ERNEST pacing in a section of cereal variety meets it's end when he lays his eyes on one box and panic snatches it for himself off the shelf in a sense based on pure gut reaction. A brand that his stomach and something more inside him advises it will quench his hunger thirst. Beholding on the front of the standing rectangular box is a miniature picture of a smiling bird specifically of that anyone was to guess is a parrot. That beak extends out like Pinocchio with three bright color bands wrapped around it. While standing before a bowl filled with a fresh rainbow colored sugar cereal drowned in milk. Hovering above in formal black text letters under the giving manufacturer company "Kellogg's" reading "FROOT LOOPS". He tosses two boxes inside his cart with a gallon of milk, some Hawaiian Punch, a few apples, and a couple packs of top ramen noodles just before checking out at the register.

In the interval, ALEX who has just arrived in his office at work decides to phone in a call to BELLE who's not only his fling in promiscuity but also his secretary and she hasn't seemed to make her way to work as of yet. Something that is improbable in her practice especially when she has consistently each day for the last two years made herself into being at the office rightfully before him. Usually taking to task his regular itineraries for the morning. Anything from making his daily coffee or tea, or taking his earlier scheduling calls. Her repeated plan like always, accept for today. Knowing this isn't normal BELLE behavior, immediately he rings her home phone at the time approximately 9:09. Without obtaining the success in having answered.

With time moving ALEX phones a friendly temp agency who employees are normally familiars with his office. With hopes that BELLE contacts him before lunch with a explanation to her no show, a probable emergency with her self or family he assumes with his conscious. But when lunchtime rolls around and he checks with his temp secretary before she goes off for lunch as she creeps in his office to deliver documents.

- Justine before you go, did I miss any calls from a woman. She could of been going under the name BELLE.

He asks in fearful hope of consideration.

- No, I don't think so...

She replies simply.

- You sure, she could of left a call back number or a "pass on".

- No I'm sure I would of remembered a call like that. Should I ?

- Just when you get back, keep an eye out on any perineal calls directed towards me. Particularly if they are from a woman, please.

- Will do ? And do you want anything I could bring back for you while I'm out.

- No thanks.

With the temp assistant leaving with the door closing behind her. ALEX curiosity now is evolving into ample fear. The feeling of defect plays his nerves, so instead of heading out for something to eat at lunch. He gets himself to the garage to his car and pays a visit to BELLE'S place where he dropped her off last night. Using the front of his fist, his knuckles pounds away at the door several times without a answer. Quickly he thinks to go around to the back door to do the same and meet the same results. When he goes back around to the front again, this time he's now met with two people. One man and one woman, they're exiting from the home directly beside BELLE'S when they both cross path. Looking for some kind of answers as to BELLE'S last whereabouts. ALEX asks the couple have they seen her in the twenty four hours outside the residence at anytime. The two negate his imposing question then move on. Once they're gone ALEX tries knocking on the door once last time before his departure. Only his bangs become a bit more intense. There still isn't a answer, naturally he tries to turns the knob and like that, one turn clockwise and it opens. He races inside her place without being detected by anyone.

When he enters he shouts out BELLE by name first in her hallway, then inside her bedroom which he notices for some reasoning doesn't seem as if she spent the night. He looks around and observes everything neatly in place, no closets cracked, dressers opened, television powered on, or even oddly her bed sheets out of order. There they were hotel styled, tucked and properly spruce. Out of the bedroom he continues on the search into the kitchen where he finds nothing and the into the living room where he flicks on the light after the realization he's been spying in darkness. When the lights comes on ALEX does discover a clue when he finds BELLE'S purse and jacket she wore last night lying on the sofa. Which does now give the explanation that she had to have at least come inside and more importantly could still be there. The findings he stumbles across encourage his inspection sense further. After a few minutes met with nothing, ALEX feels the urge to use the bathroom badly. In he walks to use the commode and while standing urinating in the dark. In his stance there's a awkward sensation, a moisture that has to be under his shoes. When he looks down he sees a dark spill not bigger than a puddle near his shoe closest to the shower tub. When he finishes, he dips his finger down in the waste. It's remains dark, so he turns the switch in the bathroom with the same finger he's dap in the spill and on the light switch there's a red smear in his fingerprint. He views the smear with his heart at the mark to race. ALEX then looks down at his finger where red the mess rests, there's no doubt that it's blood.

ALEX turns back to the spill where he originally met the blood between the toilet and shower. He sees his footprint dabbed into the thick red fluid and sees that its streaming from the tail of the shower curtain. Knowing whatever it is on the other side without saying aloud or even to his self, it will be a explanation to BELLE'S sudden disappearance. ALEX backs away from the shower with more blood scatter over the floor from his shoe trails. Drawn from the fright ALEX visions a silhouette figure behind the curtain, he conjures his fears and swallows a ton of his horrific intimidation as he slowly paces to the shower in consideration to unveil what is behind it. He clinches his hand tightly around the base space and peels back the thick plastic covering and sees what his mind was pre-accurate to before the exposure. But the revealing is far more worst than he anticipated.

There stretched out to her death from the unknown is BELLE. The tub is leveled in blood from her poor, half naked, mutilated body. The sight is enough to make you either weep or cringe in a possible heave in sickness. ALEX does neither but stand and watch in shock. Viewing BELLE'S corpse that had to be sunken to the lack of mercy to her killer. Seeing the blood scattered all over herself and everywhere in a close proximity gruesomely you would never known if she had any beauty from her facial disfigurement from a apparent beating before the joy of conquering her dearly departure, how her eyes were sprouted open as if she endured each template of pain the culprit could administer, more petrifying is very distinctly for ALEX as he kneels down and can see a hole the size of a baseball that shoots straight through her chest in a unsettling glance. A cavity size hollow where it looks to be her heart was removed grizzly by some inhumane menacing sicko. Indeed it was, just as ALEX makes his way from the bathroom after bestowing eyes on a scene like such that can't hold no comparison to the worst imagery that anyone's most sinister dream could possibly illustrate to them. There placed at the lowered torso of the girl's soulless stiff remains is a letter sealed into a off white envelope that reads on the front of it is his name in cursive letters almost as a gift. Appealing remarkably weird as to having a advantage of not being graced with not as a single drop of blood when ALEX lifts the note from the body.

He observes it in detail first then spins it to the seal when he rises on to his feet. He detaches the letter from the envelope and unfolds it for the eerie words to read in a cryptic message that sounds out simply in it's chilling approach.

" DEAR ALEXANDER GEORGE ST. CLAIR OF 2632 WISCONSIN AVENUE. WHEN READING THIS I WANT YOU TO KNOW THAT NOW THAT YOU HAVE SOMETHING OF MINES. I FELT OBLIGATED TO RETURN THE FAVOR TO YOU THE SAME. I WILL BE IN CLOSE TOUCH.

SINCERELY YOURS
122-467-899 "

Left in a space of tremble from the written word that from it's bright purpose on every line threatens ALEX existence hauntingly apparently for a reason he's unknown to. But what he does know and recognize that this executioner isn't to be trifled with after making it clear through the letter that he not only knows his full name, address, but even more wicked in the epilogue the note with his social security number as a farewell. Not to also mention his fillet work on BELLE that has her marinating in a tub of her own gore, butchered up like a helpless animal.

Coming in from the front there's some knocks at the door. With a voice and a identity to follow it " HELLO... This is the police we've got a called for this residence, open up."

ALEX eyes shoot out of his head as he fidgets while stampeding from the bathroom in dread. Choking the note in his hand, out the back he tries for his escape but that exit strategy has to be revamped noticing two suited officers beating him to the door as peeps from the rear window.

ALEX in hurry surges back to BELLE'S bedroom. Expands her window wide as he passage out fortunate enough to plant himself on the ground without taking on any suspending maneuvers. In minutes before the cops move themselves in, the door remains to be unlocked to the uninvited.

His arrival back to the office is a uneasy and unsettling one after his previous encounter that has his mind doing back flips. Waltzing through the doors before heading into his office, the secretary lets him know that a woman like he preordained before lunch has called in for a moment of conversation. Although she wasn't informed to the woman's name, she did say she would lend another call when she felt that ALEX was back into his office. He appreciates her debriefing him on his calls while he was out and he does so airy to her informing, ALEX is too uptight from the past events to worry about calls at this time, he bursts past the door into his office to ease himself down from the horror show that's he's witnessed and supposedly according to psychopathic stalker from the note that was left on his side woman's mutilated body. He's also a cast member aboard. There in his chair at his desk the only flash in sharp pictures like from a snap from a camera in and out of his mind is in remembrance of the way BELLE'S body look there in the tub at her home so malformed and disfigured. It's too much for Alex to bare as he rummages his hands stressfully through his hair as he rereads the creepy passages from the letter that was left behind by the person who's more descriptive in abnormal.

ALEX can do nothing but rely to his mind on who it is that could have done something to this caliber of sick in spite to tear him down. Or perhaps better of thought, what has he done to someone who's fierce in the likes compared to this killer to tear a whole through a female's chest. The capability of someone this sadistic wears in on ALEX knowing that whatever this person retribution for whatever it is he did isn't over and it won't be. Unless this psychopath kills him, or he gets an advantage and brings this butcher to his own demise by his own hands. Nonetheless this entire fiasco is enough to make ALEX take his own life and he probably could, if he wasn't so cowardly weak enough to fulfill that mission, and he is. His pampered journey life from catholic schools where conflicts never surpassed petty threats and finger pointing, ALEX as quiet as its kept couldn't withstand his regular doctor immunization visits without being drenched in his own jitters. How can he take on someone who's obviously has no problem without warning snatching a life no different from a reaper.

In front of him at his desk the phone at its peak volume rings continuously. The noise is so blared, ALEX complete body squirms out of his pure state of scare, wiggling womanly as it rings three times before the secretary from the outside intercom asks.

- Mr. ST. CLAIR are you going to answer or should I leave a message for you.

She says.

- No need, I have it under control. Thank you !

His aid leaves him to the call as it rings two more times before ALEX scared to oblivion lifts it off the hook and hesitantly he answers before swallowing deeply as if this is his last breath.

- HELLO !

He says to the unknown voice on the other side, that mysteriously is inhaling and exhaling over the phone seconds that feels more like minutes to him as he waits before whatever or whomever make themselves announce during the call.

- Three times... Three times I've called there looking for you. Where were you ? I got worried after lunch was over and you didn't call as usual.

The voice that surfaces over the call is ALEX'S wife CLARISSA.

- I-I got caught up into something, it must've slipped my mind.

He says.

- Well that's never happened before. It's bizarre don't you think. What was it more work.

She asks.

- No something else (staring down at the note there up the right of arm). What about you. ?

- Believe it or not I was hoping to reconcile our fight from last night, I don't know what came over me, paranoia maybe. Anyways the important thing is I was calling to make up and I wanted to take you out for dinner my treat tonight. My way of an apology. Are you free ?

She requests.

- That's fine.

He says from a feeling of stress and being out of place. She catches on to his agitation.

- Is everything alright ALEX.

She says very concerned.

- Things are fine. I-I just gotta ton of work to finish. Can we decide later on what time.

- Sure I'll drop the kids over at the babysitter and then I'll call BELLE later and leave her with the arrangements like before...hold on that wasn't BELLE who I spoke too earlier, was it ?

In from the outer desk is the substitute secretary on the intercom. She advises ALEX during the middle of his call with CLARISSA. There's an arrival of two police officers here to speak with him immediately and its urgent. He gets rid of CLARISSA instantly after hearing the words P-O-L-I-C-E utter from her mouth.
A rush to his nerves main lines him to panic. Immediately his thoughts scramble. His mind races that they've found BELLE'S body and they're on to him as a main suspect. Someone had to have seen her leave from my car last night. He's the only individual that was last seen with her, they'll pinpoint him for sure, no doubt. But wait as his conscience goes into numerous directions he realizes that he's nervous as if he has something to hide or as if he is responsible to what happened to BELLE. When he has a letter from the killer right there in his possession. The rush dissolves after his recollection item that will claim his evidence so he finally assures his secretary over the intercom.

- Send them in.

The duo of cops march in carrying a apprehending presence with them. ALEX at his desk with a sheer look of confidence greets the both of them with eloquence and then offers the both of them any beverage if they were inclined. They prefer not and they then go into full why he's expecting their company. The first cop goes on to ask.

- MR. ST CLAIR are you aware of the identity of a woman by the name of a ANNABELLE GOOD. According to our documents it says that she worked here, is that correct ?

He says.

- Yes she does, she's been here for over two years and never know her to miss a day like today either. Is something wrong.? Is she ok ?

ALEX replies very easy and calm

- MR. ST. CLAIR, MS. GOOD was found not long ago dead inside her apartment bathroom.

The cop explains.

- Are you serious, when did this happened ?

ALEX says with concern.

- Apparently last night after she had arrived home. There's hundred of clues that all point that this was a blatant homicide.

He details.

- What can I say, ANNABELLE was a beautiful worker, dedicated, and devoted. I don't know what I'd do without a woman like her. I hinted a problem earlier when she didn't arrive this morning.

ALEX explains. The two cops listen on while in seconds sharing a indifferent look at each other that involve his story. The gesture doesn't ease pass him and he asks them what's the problems when he sees that they continue again. So he asks them.

- What's the problem ?

The cops once again do the same look at each other, confused to what their interpreting amongst one another. Then the second cop who until now hasn't spoken any words walks back to his office door and locks it from the inside while saying this in the most uncomfortable, intimidating way.

- It's like this MR. ST. CLAIR because we're curious and all we want to know is the truth so I'm going ask you something and I'm only going to ask you this once and only once. Because I know...that you know the answer. So here it is. Where were you last night between eleven and midnight.

He exhorts.

- I had already left my office by ten so by midnight I was already home with my wife and she can verify that.

ALEX responds without a break of sweat.

- So what if I was to tell you MR. ST. CLAIR that I, me personally had a witness come forward and stated that she saw ANNABELLE GOOD last night between eleven and midnight going inside her apartment after departing from a red, burgundy colored vehicle.

- I don't know what to say after I had already stated my whereabouts pertaining to the hours you've asked.

ALEX states holding on to as much confidence he can. The first cop then hands the second cop who's doing the fishing a couple of photos that he neatly places in front of ALEX on his desk.

- What color car you own MR. ST. CLAIR red or burgundy ?

He asks.

- My car is red.

He answers.

- Red like the car in this photo, yes.

He asks.

- The very same.

ALEX replies nervously.

- That is your car here in this photo MR. ST. CLAIR...and there outside the last vehicle on the third row. Yes or no ?

The second cop pointing outside of ALEX'S window in the parking lot.

- Yes !

With a web of pleas and cries that he screams that they have him mistaken for another suspect. But his own admittance to his car which was said to be fingered by a witness is enough lead to have ALEX placed under arrest by the two officers and escorted out of his office for further questioning in suspicion of the murder on ANNABELLE GOOD behalf.

The beaming glow from a light reflects over ALEX'S face in a solid white background that's his mug shot when he's taken down at the station. They flash him from a front angle and both sides. He's then escorted into a single room where's there's nothing more inside but a chair and a solid black desk. It's here where the two arresting cops and a newly detective that runs down every single specific detail in the investigation murder of ANNABELLE. The investigator sits across from ALEX showing pictures of the apartment. Her main door, the kitchen, living room, bedroom, even the window that was propped open (after ALEX made his escape from), then the area more valuable in the examination a place ALEX is more than familiar with. The bathroom where he came close in contact with the gruesome that still remains in his subconscious and even more haunting him now with him being the prime suspect. The detective explains that there's fingerprints everywhere on each square inch of the spaces in the pictures shown to him and it isn't far from their analysis that these prints belong to ALEX. A main clue that's in their interest more than others is a foot print inside the bathroom that was tracked in ANNABELLE'S blood that leaked from the shower curtain on to the floor near the commode. They link this conclusion from when he was apprehended and booked. His shoes upon his booking are taken and immediately inspected by forensics experts without his knowing so.

The hounding harassment from the two cops and detective hoping by some strike of chance that may can score an confession from ALEX as he sits housed in a cave of they're merciless interrogation that lures them into a direction of unsuccessful results. There's nothing ALEX says in committal to any of their routine strategies other than repeated quotes " I don't know " and " I just want my phone call ". It's amazement his outer exterior is shelled the way it is against the law torture and it views their perception as if he can't be broken and it'll take serious evidence to crack his portraying innocence and reveal the sicko murderer they perceive him to being. Deep inside of ALEX is a worriment that is beyond description, he knows his troubles have only met a stage in origin of turmoil and far from ever being over or a that he can put behind him. He's been captured by the authorities as the main suspect in a murder and so much insight is against him even though he didn't do it, he'd still have to convict himself. Also trailing his thoughts is the mental pressure from CLARISSA'S reaction once the news is out that he and BELLE had something going on and he potentially mutilated her is enough to make him drop to the ground where his feet stand to his death. These are the bad times and he doesn't inform from the enforcement who makes it clear over and over that he isn't looking at a few years but his sentencing will round off to a decade at the most, or even natural life, his plight is looking at capital punishment with it happening in the state of Virginia in the code of 53.1-1 (premeditated murder). He's destined to be stretched out arm from arm and a needle containing the deadly three doses mainlined through his body. His only thoughts are whomever is responsible in doing this and arranging this on him is an indescribable evil.

When they see he won't be playing ball in favor to them and grow tired in the process of torment. They leave him alone for forty-five minutes to an hour before garnering him his call like he wished and pleaded.

DAISY trailing inside the back door of home from a draining day at work, slips off her shoes. Only to hear the television volume coming from the living room and then finding the kitchen in a complete mess, littered with emptied plastic wrappings and leftover bowls of cereal and milk spilled over the counter. It isn't a mystery or difference as to why things in the kitchen are so cluttered and untidy for the afternoon. Being that ERNEST is home without her company to aid behind his manly filth. But what is strange to her and attracts her attention carefully as she steps around observing are discarded package paper labeled "Ramen Noodles" spread amongst the kitchen counter and stove. And boxes of " Froot Loop" cereal close by in front of devoured bowls with leftover milk after the eating awaiting to be tended to with a sponge and suds. DAISY wonders in her curiosity although she knows all this junk had to have came from her husband. But of all of twenty-six years she's been married and another five before. She's never known him to be independent with preparing his own meals without her presence and even more particular with favoring items like cheap gourmet noodles or kids sugar cereal and apples as an preferred snack. Without delay as she tosses dirty pans in the sink, she shouts out to ERNEST as loud as possible for his recognition being that he has the television volume packed high. Blaring the commentators voice from a apparent sport game that's commanding his attention.

- ERRRNEST

She yells.

Finally driven away from the attraction of the event on television after the heightening screams to his name. He answers in mangled words and a slurred speech to her calls with crunching away down on a bowl of cereal held steady to his face while his stare in amaze at the glare picture beholding to the program.

- Yea...

She replies.

- Are you okay ?

She asks

- Cant say something wrong... I feel fantastic. Last night I shot around at the court all day long...

- Your going out on your own, I thought the doctor said you should rest plenty.

She worries.

- ... he did but I feel better and I say otherwise besides ever since I left the hospital I've had this feeling you know, a feeling I've never felt in my life. Almost like I'm invincible or I can do anything, its invigorating, I'm a kid again. I've been eating bowls of cereal since you left this morning.

He continues.

- Cereal ???

She says.

- Umm-hmm ! Froot Loops the best.

He replies.

- Since when you eat cereal Ernest, We've been married for thirty years and I can't even ponder the thought you ever eating a bowl of these " Froot Loops". And I thought you said milk gave you a gritty after taste.

- I also said it'll be a cold day in hell before someone pays a black a million dollars because he slam a ball through a hoop. And now there's this Earvin Johnson.

DAISY has no comprehension to her husband sudden reborn mannerisms. Just that they're simply and freakishly unorthodox. She cannot explain it but does looks on as he shouts in countdown for the last bit of remainder seconds of the latest Laker game winding down in victory celebration.

- FIVE, FOUR, THREE, TWO, ONE.

The eruption of overjoy from the audience televised game rumbles in volume through the living space. With DAISY caring to upkeep the kitchen and ERNEST face to face in the palm of two pass times for a man. One being television while the other is sports. RING...RING goes the phone on the opposing side of the kitchen where DAISY runs water from the faucet at the sink over dirty dishes. It doesn't ring once more as she snags it off the hook for a answer.

- Hello !

She says. Right after there's a woman voice that's automated that responds.

" This is a call from Department of Corrections, will you accept a call from ..."

The automated voice then ascends into surprisingly ALEX'S that is inserted from the process during the call. DAISY drops her jaw in split reaction between fright and anger when its apparent her son is in jail.

- ALEX what is going on ?

Bold she asks.

- Mom I'll explain to you later, I need to talk to dad right now, where is he ?

Deep in frustration she says.

- Hold on...

Grasping her hand covering the speaker over the phone. DAISY shouts over ERNEST in his chair.

- ERNEST its ALEX I think he's in jail.

She cries.

- WHAAAT ?

In a steam of excite he lifts himself from his seat into the kitchen and steals the phone from his wife and takes over the call. With her breathing down his back in concern.

- ALEX what's going on. Where are you ?

- Uh... Uh I'm down by a dozen and it might rain.

He responds in code.

- I'll get my coat.

He says and hangs up the phone.

ONE HOUR LATER...

Two sets of casual black shoes march at a persistence alongside each other, with one pair a step ahead of the other. Heading to a destination that seem to rest in the pits of a dungeon being how the steps they parade echo the surrounding they past from the hard, cold concrete ground. A melody of jangled keys also follow them in as they proceed in the dim setting.

It's only a few seconds more until the walking ends and they arrive at the object intending.

There seated on a bed to his lonesome behind bars caressing his neck is ALEX, its plain he's deep in irritation from stress. When the two figures make themselves known at his cell he stands at a desperate attention at face to them. A voice is heard.

- LETS GET THIS OVER WITH. Get him out of there.

The first individual is a prison guard unlatching his cell to be opened in arrangements to the demanding tone, and the other who's voice clamors in fuss. Is a mature older man packed together in a suit with no tie and with the final few buttons on his shirt loosened to the top like he was in a hurry. Once the gate opens he hugs ALEX like a old friend and asks if he's alright, then moves the way for him to step out of his cell. His name is ROYAL BURNS and his business with ALEX is that he's the ST.

CLAIR'S family attorney and has been for years being that he and ERNEST are college buddies.

With money being put up for his bail and BURNS taking over as his active attorney. ALEX is finally assisted into being released and when upon his exit he's met with his father ERNEST outside. The three get into his vehicle and off they are from the department a relief for now off of ALEX shoulders.

During the drive he explains everything to both his father and BURNS to what happened. From his ongoing relationship with BELLE who's also his secretary, dropping her off the night before, and then showing up to her apartment where he discovered her dead body and then panicking once the arrival of the police, the fleeing from the scene leaving behind evidence the can pin him as the killer even with his innocence.

- You should had never went to that apartment, now they all have the excuse to pin you as the murderer regardless your admittance or not. This is going to cost more than a pretty penny to keep you out of prison.

ERNEST says while chopping his teeth down into a apple. ALEX looks on strange but briefly at his father.

- I know dad, I only went because I was worried that something like this had happened, it still rubs me wrong that my worst thought came to be true. What are we going to do ROYAL ?

ALEX replies.

- Well first you need to write down and think of anyone and everything that has some type of grudge against you in anyway whether it comes from you, your dad, or mother. I can't get you off if we can't pin this on someone else, and I can't guarantee you won't spend a portion of agonizing time in jail if you don't have any evidence that can prove this was the work from someone else and not you.

He informs. It's been a while and his interrogation adventure the cops took him on in front seat and gave him a mind to forget almost. Immediately a thought of gold strikes him that's more than worthy goods that's significant in gaining his freedom like BURNS advises.

- The letter... Holy shit the letter. Those cops pestering me for hours must of knocked it out of my mind. I literally forgot about it. I think it's still left on my desk from when they came down to apprehend me.

He says.

- Letter, letter, wait a minute what letter ?

ERNEST asks.

- Yea what do you mean letter ?

BURNS asks too.

- The letter on BELLE'S body when I found her there in the tub at the apartment. It was signed and had my name on the front of it, like whoever left it wanted me to find it there. The crazy motherfucka even signed it sincerely with my social security number.

He replies.

- Do you have it, where is it now ?

BURNS asks.

- It cant be nowhere else but my office where I left it when they came to arrest to me.

ERNEST picks up some speed after a red light and head on to the freeway in direction to ALEX'S office in desires to retrieving this letter. When they get there, on the desk it is and he shows it to both of them. BURNS carefully inspects it and reads it through, then tells ALEX.

- You had a letter like this that proves your innocence and you didn't make it a priority to show the police off hand.

BURNS confusingly asks.

- I don't fucking know, I was scared to death, I had just left her place where it all happened...

He replies.

- Do you think its creditable ?

ERNEST asks.

- Its hard to tell... You can't spring a note to the cops after a arrest in investigation. It won't convince anyone to its validity. They'll have a pre-conception that your lying. But I can send this to a lab, and have them take a look at it. There could be prints other than ALEX'S on it.

BURNS carefully folds the letter into a napkin attempting his best to not leave his fingerprints behind, he then gently shoves the note into his jacket pocket. ERNEST who still doesn't know what to make of all what's going on, sends more question to ALEX in hopes for a more detailed explanation.

- So you dropped her off the night before. How long was it until you found out she was dead ?

ERNEST says.

- Today around lunch, and its all that's been on my mind ever since. How her body looked ? Every time I blink my eyes there it is like a photo in my head, you know the bastard carved her heart out. Literally !

ALEX replies. While ERNEST and BURNS stand there in disgust with no words to say after his last statement that you can tell sends them in sickening displease.

- Did they at least find it...

BURNS asks

- They never said while they held me. I don't know...

Next BURNS advises for the both of them to invest quickly in twenty-four security as a precaution measure. Being that there's a deranged killer twisted enough to do the things ALEX has said and have personal information on him and where his family reside, he needs to be on guard at all times. A strike summons on him that reminds him of CLARISSA and previous plans she made before he was accosted several hours by cops at the precinct.

BURNS takes off while they're at the building assuring he'll be in touch with the two of them once he gets results on from the note and more specifics about the case from the investigation. Meanwhile ALEX and ERNEST trail over to ALEX'S home, its been hours since he last spoke to his wife CLARISSA who has been on the outside of the terror to what he has been undergoing in the last twenty-four hours. Shoving his key through the rear door he settles himself in preparation to her expected moody outrage. But that's nearly irrelevant once he opens his door and finds several investigators and patrolman in uniform inspecting his kitchen and basement like a robbery had been ensued.

- What the hell is this ?

He yells.

- What's going on ?

ERNEST follows.

Expectantly angered to this surprise. ALEX with his father close by begin to cause commotion to the authorities as they carry on in his vicinity that he had no knowledge of. He goes in at them cursing, shouting, and using a variety of profanity at the cops who seems to be there as if they belong, and they do. According to a warrant a fellow uniform brandishes arrogantly to a hostile ALEX which gives them the liberty to exercise a thorough search of his entire home being that he's a primary suspect in a homicide. Now relieves him of his " hissy fit" behavior like a bucket of water that's been thrown on to him. His reasoning now is because potentially his wife CLARISSA may now be aware of the situation without him explaining first. But he disposes that thought speedy when he sees there in the living room his young son and daughter standing in the middle floor seeming to be out place and unknown to all the busy with police going on. Naturally as a father he rushes to their aid with then reciprocating in response with dozens of questions such as "Dad, the police are here ". He shoots back with his own curiosity with only one question for them to direct him to.

- Where's mommy ?

He asks.

His young son BRADY, only four answers typical to how a four year old would react to a question like the ones he was asked. Looking over ALEX, his father just about to his left over in the hall near the stairs he points to his mommy. In signal to her wanted whereabouts, ALEX follows his son finger in direction and spots his wife cornered with a detective who from looking on, mentions a few words before stepping into the kitchen.

ALEX wastes no time and heads over to his wife CLARISSA, and right of way he knows that there's a problem and he can see it right in her face. He knows that there's nothing he can really do in comfort when your woman's home is being overran by the police. So he approaches her with the deepest apologies for his troubles and allowing them to be brought into their home, their family home.

- CLARISSA please hear me out, I'm sorry for all of this. But I'm telling you I'm innocent of all this, you have to believe me.

He explains.

- I guess you also expect me to believe that your innocent of this too.

She responds.

It's documented papers that come from forensics that reveal that BELLE'S body from mouth and vaginal region both contained DNA from a male gender. Now while under the custody at the local precinct the police took swabs of saliva and prints with ALEX consent. Those results regarding the DNA belonging to a male, belongs to ALEX. She shows him the paper and before he can explain, she shouts out in pain and hurt for him to leave from the house at that second. And she says it so loud that everyone overhears from the police and detectives rummaging through their home invading it and their family's privacy and even more serious are the kids as they sit near looking on troubled while ERNEST catering to the children's attention but also who cant help to watch the disgruntlement between the two as well.

- Who gave you this ?

He screams.

Looking over the papers in search for who could be the messenger delivering intel on him like that.

- I want you out of my house right now.

She replies.

Then storms past him in retrieving her kids away from ERNEST with looks to bound herself up the stairs. This angers ALEX. And demands for her to give him an explanation, the cops see things growing more and more wrong so they quickly intercept and demand for ALEX to abide by his wife commands. He erupts in anger toward the police being that they're intercepting between his wife, CLARISSA manages to escape upstairs once the cop confrontation with ALEX occurs. They advise him to calm down and when he begins to match them all as the culprits to the critical documents evening heightened in his animosity. Before you know it as ERNEST tries to step in, its too late before ALEX balls power in his fist and takes a shot at the nearest blue uniform in sight. Wrong in his actions, they restrain him to the floor very tough and physically. ERNEST does all he can calling out against the force.

- That's my son !

Luckily for the both of them, the cops gave him pass and didn't charge him for reacting with his volatile behavior toward them. But he was detained in handcuffs and placed inside a squad car for a short duration until they felt his frustration had passed on to a more tolerable state.

When they feel he's more relaxed from his tantrum after finishing their trampling through his family's home. They release ALEX from the handcuffs as exception to ERNEST who they later realize to be a patriot of the govern first-hand and into his responsibility, who stands by in concern. They leave him with a advisory as a father to get his son home to a place where he isn't going to be set off like minutes earlier. That'll eventually lead him on more charges and can ultimately worsen his situation even further. ERNEST agrees and shields ALEX right away gravely taking the cops advice.

- Don't worry about any of that.

He comments.

ALEX on the other hand who's brought down from his past tirade. Displays a facial demeanor enforce with anger still, but with a mind of calm in compromise to not wanting to undergo the extreme authority measures he was succumbed to. Drifting to the car as all the police look on at him standing firm in front of his home as if its under their jurisdiction now, guardians of protection for CLARISSA. Looking back ALEX views this in hatred and in wish he could do something but he doesn't, in glimpses he catches peeping neighbors looking on as sneaks from behind their window drapes suspecting poking fun at his foolish ordeal. Just as he's off, there's a realization ALEX has as he pictures the bold and arrogant police force occupying his territory in similarity to a mob. It's the envelope and document that he retrieved from CLARISSA where she exposed his infidelities that he had thought came from the dealings of the scummy officers. Lying on his lawn no more than a few steps away from his front door. Breaking away from his dad in committal to getting inside the car he surges in desperation for them and in low voice he tells his father.

- I have to get my papers.

Its instant detention the police act on to constrain him from getting any closer to the house. A couple of the officers shoot toward him with intentions to do serious damage while others place hands on what appears to be their standard issue weapons but really stun guns to gentle him down once more for his good. Before the rumble engages, ERNEST at the top his lungs yells out.

- ALLOW THE BOY HIS PAPERS.

The fellow officers who submitted to them the advise statement hears his fathers message and then settle the tensions from his team of crude patriots with.

- SETTLE DOWN HE'S ONLY GETTING HIS PAPERS GUYS.

The police bind themselves back out of a mode driven in defense. And ALEX swipes his papers from the grass and into his possession before he heads off from his home where he's experience complete disruption and dysfunction at it's finest never to be seen before, he had been made a criminal, a lowlife, every accusation he's been charged with by the police. It's unimaginable to him that all of this is playing out in his life.

While ERNEST behind the wheel in attempt to shed light in sympathy towards his son at this time in need. He passes on to him in comfort to not to worry and that they'll soon figure all this out. From the situation, the murder, this twisted killer, and in all how to clear his name of everything without even fathom of having to serve out any sentence rotting away inside a pathetic cell. ALEX who's listens on in remaining disappointment finds himself looking down back at the documents there in his laps with grass green covered on most of it. He skims through one paper with the inscription matching his DNA. His eyes overlook it some more and right as he passes that sheet, something small grabs his eye. When he brings it back, there it is at the bottom of the page. It's the initials "RR". It's weird because ALEX senses that he's seen those exact wordings on some other document recently and he believes it could be that note from the sicko.

- Oh shit !

He says.

- What... What's wrong ?

- I need to call BURNS dad right of way. And we need a private investigator now. Hopefully he can catch some clues for all of this to make sense. You have anyone in mind ?

- I have one...

He says.

Staring oddly ALEX looks at his father as he eats away at a apple that he never spot before as his documents claimed his attention until now.

- I thought you hated apples.

He asks.

- I did.

He responds.

Once ALEX arrives to his parents house accompanied with his father in the late hours of the night. He heads straight to the phone and dials BURNS number. Meanwhile ERNEST prepares himself a bowl of cereal and raids inside the living area, after flicking on the television in search of a daily basketball game. ALEX has no success in reaching BURNS so he leaves a urgent message on his voice mail machine to contact him as soon as possible once he hears the message. When he finishes he hangs up the phone and joins his dad in the living room but he doesn't leave the kitchen with being a blind eye to his dad's new indulgence in kids cereal.

ALEX shoves his self into a chair with stress escaping from his breath as he leans backwards with the weight of all his problems in his lap.

- Things will work themselves out, push comes to shove we'll tell ROYAL settle the case in your favor and we'll pay her family in confidentiality. So don't worry, this isn't anything to worry about.

He expresses.

- Yea but more than that, this prick with a message and not a face scares me even more. What's the investigator friend you have in mind ?

ALEX responds.

- Guy by the name CUOCO...

ERNEST says almost incoherently as he slurps down a spoonful of cereal milk down his throat rapidly.

- CUOCO ? I hope you don't mean VIC CUOCO. That cheesy ass guinea grease ball guy with the soap commercial where he was a ex detective who always has his " Ear to the street". He's a gimmick for dollars, dad.

ALEX cries.

- He is a character, no doubt about that. But he does have a knack in finding just about anyone and only in a few hours a friend assured me. Which is what we need to catch our pest. I'll pay CUOCO, he finds the guy, and we turn him over to the police for the murder that they'll know you didn't commit with the letter identifiable from his handwriting and everything will be over. Finished !

ERNEST replies.

- I hope so...

ALEX responds.

A molecule of the seconds after their previous discussion about this pre-hired private eye. On the television brightening up the living room with its glare summons CUOCO'S own infomercial styled cut runs. A touching feeling of coincidence circles ALEX mind as the thirty-second t.v spot showcases the rough cut inspector voicing why his meager advertisement would be any value to interested customers. That's in notoriety all over town and heavily prone to be shown during mid day and late into the night. Fixed at the television until the measly broadcast ends, ALEX sits there well adjusted into the chair until he drifts off into sleep.

4.CHAPTER

The next day ALEX with his father ERNEST appearing bright early in the office of CUOCO'S as potential clientele for his expert investigative services seated side by side before his desk. They fill him in on their ordeal and why they've came to him, he listens on and then asks after.

- So uh where's this letter by this maniac at ?

CUOCO asks.

- It's with my attorney, he's checking for prints and whether or not they belong to someone within the system. I can take you to him if your skeptical about this whole thing.

ALEX informs.

- No, no, no don't worry about any of that. I'm way convinced by your story that your telling me the truth and I appreciate it, one thing about Italians MR. ST-CLAIR you should know it isn't any work to spot a liar and his bullshit, once he's opened his mouth, ya get me. I believe you kid, and to show I'm sympathetic to you and your little problem. I'm taking your case on but it isn't just because my gut feeling never lies. But also it sounds like you gotta psycho on your hands, and there's one thing that scratches me the wrong way even more than a jig and its a twisted, menace, cold hearted fucking psycho. They have no morals, which is why this beloved country is sinking into a hole of shit as we speak and pardon my language. But you don't do those things to a woman like you described this perp did and get away with it, not from a guy like me VICTOR CUOCO. You get what I'm saying. Believe me I take down jerk-offs like that in my pajamas in my nightmares let me tell ya'.

He replies.

- I'm with you...

ALEX says.

- Good because I'm going find this low life, two-bit prick. And you know what I'm do to him.

He says.

- What's that ?

ERNEST asks

- I'm going to stomp a fucking mud hole the size of the fucking capital downtown in his ass. And when I'm finished, I'm gonna turn the sick fuck over to the cops so they can see what I did to him, and then I'm gonna tell them I'm responsible for the shithead looking like shit, and then I'm gonna tell them they can charge me with whatever the fuck they want so long as I get to kick the son of the bitch right in his ass so he'd fly into the fucking cell. How's that sound to you ?

CUOCO explains.

- Sounds pretty good, that's just what we need for this catastrophe.

ERNEST asks.

- It sounds pretty fucking good to me too. Don't mind me, I get like this when I get worked up. But this is good, it gets the juices flowing when your dealing with a bonafide nut like this. But first we have to deal with my wages, so look this over. Sign this agreement, and we can start from there.

ERNEST who's playing benefactor, whips out his check book and writes out a check toward CUOCO directly after him and ALEX place their signatures below both document papers. When they've held up their end of the deal on paper, they hand it over to CUOCO as he makes sure everything is intact thoroughly. Being joyous that they've solidified an authentic agreement on both ends of their party. CUOCO extends his hands out to both ALEX and ERNEST all in motion of good business.

- Well everything looks good and we have that end of the business wrapped or how we say it in my family " avvolto ". Grazie !

He says.

- I just hope we can catch this guy quick, fast, and a hurry.

ALEX replies.

- Hey, and I don't mean any offense. But hope is for pussies if you could excuse my expression. I'm VIC CUOCO and there's no piece of shit scumbag out there that I can't find, ok… now let's get outta here. We got flies to stomp.

First stop that CUOCO wants to trace is BELLE'S apartment where everything went down. His intentions are strictly to get a feel for any clues that were left behind and untracked by the police who he feels are piss poor at any investigation in comparison to his ample ability. Once there he sees that her place has been caution taped all over and marked as an important investigation ground, where no one unless authorized with police should trespass, any violators can be tried in the court of law on serious repercussions. Except those precautions listed by the authorities go inside a trash can when dealing with the likes of CUOCO. While standing outside the very window ALEX used to make a wrenching escape from as the police nearly had him jammed in while he was inside BELLE'S apartment and discovered the grizzly scene. CUOCO advises the father and son to keep a close and tight eye for the police as he sneaks inside her apartment from the outside window.

- Now I'm going in, I'll only be ten minutes nothing any further alright, I want you too stand here and keep an eye out. You feel any cops on our tail, you get your ass in your car and speed off as fast as you can because if you get pinched I can't protect you then. I have your number, I'll call you, and we'll meet up later. Understand.

He says.

- Ay, you sure this is safe that's a lot of cautionary tape. What if it's a uniform inside.

ERNEST asks.

- Look, let me do my business and just do me a fucking a favor and keep your fucking eyes peeled and your skirt down, alright. Remember I said only ten minutes.

He answers. While covering his rubber gloves over his hands with the grip on his lips carefully. As ALEX and ERNEST duo there by the window. CUOCO props his self up nearest to the window, easing it to be raise by pressing the glass in a upward position, its a minor struggle but he prevails and manages to get himself through on to the other side. ALEX and ERNEST look on as he squirms in and immediately after they ditch CUOCO'S plan as lookouts for his illogical arrangement for his task.

- You think we should wait for this idiot, dad.

ALEX says.

- Hell no, besides you can't afford any more attention as it is, last thing we need is you to get pinched again. Let's wait in the car. When he's finished we'll honk the horn for him from on the other side of the street.

ERNEST replies.

They march away from outside the window space, carefully trying no to be detected by any neighbors or pedestrians trolling along the sidewalk. As they make themselves to the car.

CUOCO who's now has feet planted inside BELLE'S homicide tape occupied apartment. Wonders himself around attentively in silence flickering a skinny flashlight around for a better enhanced look. Trying his best not to be detected in anyway by strangers or nearby cops that plague the awful crime scene. He allows himself into every space in the home. First into the living room, brandishing his light before childhood photos of ANNABELLE around fancy frames, expensive appearing love seats, and worthy sculptures crafted into glass animals. These valuable trinkets catches CUOCO'S eye sorely so much that he decides to helps himself to them by placing a few into his jacket pocket uncaring that they're previous possessions of a woman who had her heart grotesquely removed from her chest, a few feet away in the bathroom.

After his takings in the living room, its the bedroom he pillages through next. Stepping as quiet as can be taking form to a cat burglar. His eyes switch directly to her dresser that holds assortment personals for a princess. From anything feminine to perfume, flip-out mirrors, nail polish, hair curlers, brushes, but the prize of them all for a blunt thief. A lock box in the shape of a tiny chest trunk that rested on four pint-sized stomps that served as legs. It resembled a accessory for a doll or girl figure toy that had been kept in its uniqueness for years and years. It wouldn't matter for long though, as CUOCO got his hands on to it with numerous wiggles for a pry open. There it is enclosed inside premium jewelry. Diamond encrusted rings, rock size diamond earrings that look excessively costly, pearl necklaces that stretch out like never ending pasta. Along with a few gold tennis bracelets and one solid thick gold necklace that doesn't shy CUOCO to holding up to the room light as it shimmers in a way that tells you that there's nothing flawed about it. He packs it all up back into the chest for his further taking.

- Those two chumps and dead bitch can consider this a bonus for my extra strides in hard work.

He says giggling.

Meanwhile outside the vehicle ALEX and ERNEST stare nervously on and on at that window CUOCO manage to break himself in. Hoping every second he'd appear out of especially now that he's setting in on eight minutes pass the ten he insisted he'd be finished. ALEX every two or three minutes or so peeping down at his watch growing frustrated at the wait finally he says.

- What the hell is taking him so long, its eight minutes past the ten he said he'd be out of. We're going to have go in there in get him.

ALEX says.

- Let's just wait a few minutes more, he isn't out in another ten we'll leave. Maybe the police found him in the apartment.

ERNEST replies.

ALEX spots a phone booth, a block up the street. He gets he urge to call BURNS on the results from yesterday on their main lead with the note.

- I gotta call BURNS.

He says. Withdrawing his wallet from his back pocket uncomfortably in search for his personal card that holds his contacts numbers on the front of them.

- Go on ahead, I'll keep an eye out for this jackass.

ERNEST replies.

ALEX slams the door tightly shut after he part ways momentarily from the car with his dad awaiting inside. He sprints a few blocks up from where everything takes place. There at booth with his card in hand, he dials his number and waits as it rings. After three rings there's an answer and its from BURNS.

- Good afternoon, this is ROYAL speaking, how can I assist you ?

He exhorts professionally.

- BURNS its me ALEX. Did you hear anything back on those results ?

ALEX asks.

- I been trying to get in contact with you and father since this morning. I got your call last night. I called your parents home a hour ago and your mother said you and your father was gone. Anyways, I need you both down here at the office, my friends said they'll have everything for me in a half of hour. Get your ass down here now, pronto...wait, wait, wait...

BURNS exhorts. Before his pause there's another phone ringing and it seems BURNS has taken the call. He words a few mumbled words that go unheard and then he resumes his conversation with ALEX.

- ALEX, I have to take this call. Get down here in a hurry, I'll see you when you do.

He says.

- I'll be there. Thanks again.

ALEX slams the phone on to the hook and out of the booth he goes.

CUOCO back inside BELLE'S apartment practices more of that inspecting for clues and leads. With all the chattel goods he has sticky fingers for. He checks his watch and sees that its way past ten minutes like he promised but ensues for more luck in his search.

- If this broad is big on junk and jewels, this bitch has to have some bucks lying around here somewhere.

CUOCO saying to himself. He crosses over to drawers after his come up on the ice he's found. In those there's nothing worth mentioning or peeping over twice. There is panties from BELLE he grows a awkward attachment to, sniffing some before placing them back where they were originally. Lastly he rams through her walk in closet, checking the top that's filled with endless pairs of stilettos and heels. The racks are cluttered with women's outfits and clothing. He bends on his knees to check the depths of the floor which are too spaced with shoes and other miscellaneous items. While shoving a few shoe boxes out of his way. CUOCO comes across a letter that must've sat inside one of the boxes until now. It's been open previously and inside of it is a ordinary drug store appreciation card. He snaps its open and reads the message, at the bottom there's an additional message that he reads out loud to himself with his eyes gazed over the words. It reads;

" Hey Belle I wish you a happy birthday and being in my life. I hope this five thousand dollars is well worth a gift that is to your consideration.

Love ALEX"

When hearing the words five grand, CUOCO'S breath almost deserts him. He looks around himself as if the generous amount had escaped him when opening the letter. He does the same to the envelope, there isn't anything there and it never was. It doesn't shatter him too bad but it does passes on to him the thought on what kind of man is able to give a woman five thousand dollars for a gift ? His observation gives him the perception that ALEX and ERNEST has access to way more money then he perceived.

He tosses the letter and rounds up the case stuffed with the elegant property. He can't go outside revealing what he swiped shoved into his shirt so blatantly obvious, so he finds a heavy metal box under BELLE'S sink filled with tools and he buries the case carefully under some old wrenches and screw drivers. When surging from the window without miraculously being detected by anyone. Outside CUOCO finds himself by his lonesome and gets the idea that ALEX and ERNEST had to have left him behind. He stands in the alley space where they all stood before he entered inside. All peeping and looking around as if he's lost. A few honks from a car horn aimlessly is made that eventually gets his attention from across the street where the two sit and watch from the car window views.

CUOCO fleeing across the street in a stagger due to the heavy tool box he carries, makes his way back into the back seat as ERNEST starts the engine and pulls off. ALEX who's seated in the passenger seat irritated from CUOCO having them wait longer than he anticipated demands to know what dragged his observation.

- It's been almost forty-five minutes what was it that took so long. Did you at least find anything ?

ALEX asks.

- Not a fucking thing. By the time I made it in, a cop inside heard me come through the window and spent twenty minutes in paranoia checking the place up and down. By the time he was finished, I had realize my time had went over.

CUOCO replies.

- What you got in the toolbox ?

ERNEST asks. CUOCO pauses in nervous and thinks to say the first thing that comes to mind.

- I just took it as a gag you know, to fool the cops if they caught me while in the house. I could say I'm maintenance or something. Where we going ?

CUOCO says.

- I have to talk to my lawyer, he said he'd have the results of the prints any minute now.

ALEX explains.

- That's good...we need all the help we can get.

Arriving at BURNS office soon after, ALEX knocks on his door and before it opens there's a voice that can be heard. It comes from BURNS as he speaks in the midst of a conversation from his cordless phone on the other side. He swings the door open for them to come inside his cozy office, a room that's impossible to fit a couch into and gestures words through his fingers as he continues to speak on the phone for them all to take a seat. ALEX and ERNEST squeeze themselves first into the only two chairs at his desk which leaves CUOCO still standing, the look on his face is bummed out and agitated but he sucks it up and just stands leaning by a shelf of books in the corner. ALEX behind his seat looks at BURNS who by the sound of his conversation during his phone call seems that it has involves him and his case. He follows BURNS every move from the room with ERNEST doing the same as well. Both tense at what the discussion deals in. It's only a few minutes as BURNS notions to end the call, so when he does. In a rush ALEX asks.

- Is everything alright ?

- For you... No

BURNS says.

- Why, what's going on ?

ERNEST asks while slouching indifferent in his seat.

- Well my boy it looks like after that phone call your dangling between the lines of both good and worst.

BURNS exhorts.

- Good and worst ?

ALEX reiterates.

- According to the legal defense team inclined from a JEREMIAH WELLS. The WELLS of WELLS ICE COLD CREAM the largest ice cream chain in all of twenty three states as a conglomerate in these United States of America. Is offering not only top dollar for his attorney, but I'm afraid your attorney, myself in referencing. An whopping fee of one point five million dollars in exchange that his party and mines comes to an agreement with the judge that you get the needle in death for what you did to his little girl.

He explains.

- Are you going to take it ?

ERNEST asks.

- Yea…are you because you know damn well I didn't do this, any of this. I'm being trumped up. You saw the fucking letter.

ALEX states.

- Well that's what you say, I do this for a living kid, and no offense ERNEST there's way too much evidence against him for me to even believe him. But…I'm a lawyer and we as lawyers don't tell propositions especially if its concerning one point five millions dollars. Unless I had already thought to take it up and I didn't.

BURNS says.

- What the fuck am I going to do ?

ALEX replies. Throwing his face into his hands.

- I don't know what your going to do but I know what you need to do. Because if you didn't do it, you not only need to make me believe you had nothing to do with it, but come trial that jury the same…that is if you don't plan on cooking by the chair. I suggest you can start by finding this fellow who goes by the alias "R.R.".

ALEX lifts his head in a hint to an idea that's struck him and digs into his pocket and brings out a folded paper. While ERNEST and CUOCO look on in interest after BURNS name drops the initials.

- " R.R " like on this paper CLARISSA showed to me last night.

He says. Pointing and showing BURNS from across his desk to the printed letters poking out from below the document in solid black ink like a signature or sort.

- Yea just like on this note too. Brace yourself on this next tip because when referencing this fellow I actually have this Mr. " R.R" name in official and it's...

CUOCO sounds out over BURNS name reading from a torn paper.

- RONALD RAZOR. And his street name is pronounced "DOUBLE R" not "R.R". It's kind of like a black play on words, you get it.

CUOCO laughs

- And you are ?

BURNS asks.

- My friend's call me VIC, but sense I don't know you, just call me by my last for short. It's CUOCO.

He says.

- Well I appreciate you finishing my sentence MR.CUOCO. But for future notice while your in my office, my friends may haven't told you but newcomers raise their hand to talk when I'm speaking.

BURNS says.

- You don't say ?

He replies.

- I do, I make the rules, and have no problem instructing them out. So if you don't mind...

With coming into contact with BURNS arrogant lip it boils tension in CUOCO and over his face.

BURNS then informs ALEX and ERNEST that his friends who came up with the prints also did him another favor into getting a few copies of RONALD RAZOR'S file. When he can't get his hands on it and feeling that he had to have misplace it. He calls for his secretary to bring it in for him, as they wait. BURNS recollects on the name CUOCO and realizes that he's the private eye from the commercial.

- CUOCO... Wait ! Aren't you the private eye guy with the sleazy commercials. I tell you to hire a investigator and you two hire this snook.

BURNS says. He laughs hysterically extended into a few minutes that sets CUOCO'S boil into a risen flame of hate and beginning to grow more and more as he stare without any verbal reaction to BURNS and his offensive remarks to his reputation. A subtle knock at the door comes and it's his secretary, BURNS shouts at the door at the top of his lungs.

- ENTER.

She does with the file in her arms, excusing herself if her arrival brought any interruption to their meeting and discussions. CUOCO'S eyes catches her first as she moves passed him once she enters, his natural reactions is of her womanly frame peeping enthusiastically at her behind. The secretary goes over to his desk and places the file into BURNS hands swiftly and then heads back out from the door from where she came in after he thanks her graciously. Just before she exits, she passes CUOCO only this time she's one with his eyes on the way out and she catches his winks at her seductively. It's common for a attractive women to receive sexual flirtations from men and ignore the embarrassment but she does different in this case. When CUOCO ticks his eye at her , her first motion is to not pay him or his weak advances any mind but then her instincts picks her brain and she catches herself realizing he's familiar. So she says to him.

- Wait haven't I seen you or met you before.

- I don't think so darling, but let me write my number down for you and maybe we can arrange something this weekend. I'll come by and pick you up. How's that sound ?

CUOCO responds confidently.

- Now I remember it wasn't a date, your that dumbass from those commercials. With those pimp lines where you say " I keep my ears to the street". It's socially common that guineas hate niggas but yet why do they insist on acting like them I'll never know.

The room bursts into laugher outstandingly from BURNS as he cackles freakishly weird and uncomfortably from his seat as his secretary exits and slams the door behind her. CUOCO is crushed from the sassy secretary's roasting denigrations and the only thing he can think to do is turn away mouthing the words after "skank" then from his view directly at BURNS as he stands laughing away raising from his seat. CUOCO turns his head to the wall and snaps his neck from being so tensed and he tightens his right fist so snug that the bone in it too cracks real smooth and goes nearly unheard.

BURNS circles around his desk with the folder file in hand and spreads it open all the while still in chuckle from what had just occurred and begins to read out the last address known to "DOUBLE R".

- Here's the guy address five-one...

But before he can finish standing between ALEX and ERNEST he turns to CUOCO who's in the chair behind him feeling sunken as he feels to have his ego scorn from embarrassment. BURNS carries on with his joking and hacking cackle until CUOCO can take no more having to be the center of amusement, ejecting from his chair for only one instance to his reaction then...BOPPPP!

CUOCO sends a straight hand to BURNS mouth with so much force behind it. It sends him in a aerial maneuver across his desk past both ALEX and ERNEST leaping from their seats in frightening amazement. His leap over knocks dozens of his files and papers on to the floor from his body rattling over them like a weightless object. CUOCO finishes the address reading on the account BURNS isn't capable to, with him being one with the floor behind his desk, its unimaginable the pain he's just endured from the shot he took.

- Five-one-thirty, fourth street, northeast. Hope you get the message. I'd look like an asshole to have a puny little fuck like you to treat a CUOCO with the up most of disgrace.

With everything happening so fast and them hopping out of their chairs after. ALEX lunges over BURNS desk as he gathers himself from the floor and back onto his feet. His face is covered in a red, pink shadow of pain. His mouth is splattered with a glob of blood that he ends up spatting on his floor. ERNEST looks in disgust. BURNS yells out in dizziness.

- I think he knocked out my fucking teeth.

He says.

- Let me see...

- ALEX asks.

He grins with his eyes filling with tears from the suffering and his mouth bruised in the entire lip section badly and his mouth appearing gutty red because of his gashed flesh throbbing in view. When he spreads open his mouth so they all can see. His rows of choppers lay missing two spots, in both section from top to bottom. Grinning there he looked as if someone couldn't quite solved a word block puzzle only with his teeth. CUOCO instantly blurts out in laughter in retribution.

- Good god he did knock out your fucking teeth.

ERNEST says.

With blood seeping in waterfalls down his chin. He turns to his mirror in the corner and pictures his reflection in it with his missing dentures and it turns him painfully sad. He steps forward for a closer view and he feels something hard on the bottom of his shoe. He looks down and lifts his feet and its his tooth he's trampling on. CUOCO continues on in his comical spectacle, grueling and rubbing it in even more.

- What do you call a guy with a big fucking mouth against a guy with a big fucking fist... I call him TOOTHLESS.

ALEX does his best to hide his cackling expressing the moment does to his admittance has humor even though he wishes to veil it as much as possible. Before BURNS sees, and he notices with wrath.

BURNS salvages both teeth off his floor and observe them one by one. With CUOCO raining on his parade horribly. In rushes his secretary once again aiding to see what had occurred after hearing the commotion.

- Is everything alright ROYAL.

When he turns to her and she sees his bridgework disfigurement. Immediately she says.

- Oh my god, I'll call the paramedics.

ALEX interrupts and reaches over to BURNS in pursuit to dial instead.

- I'll do it.

- NO ....

BURNS says in a deep tone. Grabbing ALEX'S wrist with blood smeared all over his hand intercepting him from attempting to dial on his office desk phone. ALEX pauses and just looks at him as he goes into a rampage fit demanding they all leave at the moment cursing and shunning them spatting blood everywhere as his speech makes a turn to deficiency now that he's lost a few pearly whites from a devastating strike to his mouth trap.

- GET THA FUCK OUTTA MY OFFICE ALL OF YOU RIGHT NOW. ERNEST FUCK YOU, FUCK YOUR SON I HOPE HE FUCKIN ROTS IN JAIL WITH A DICK IN HIS ASS. I FORFEIT IM NOT DEFENDING YOU, I WANT YOU AND THIS GREASY PIECE OF SHIT OUT OF MY OFFICE RIGHT NOW BEFORE I CALL THE COPS.

He screams in a clamorous disturbance. ALEX and ERNEST step back toward the door as they look up, close and personal to his charade in anger that in reality is no good for them and their first hand plight. ERNEST tries his best as a last minute chance to redeem everything wrong that has occurred, humbling asking for BURNS to calm down.

- BURNS come on we need you, lets settle this out.

He levels with him. It does no good and in seconds BURNS screams out again and rips his phone from the wall and sends it directly at him.

- NO FUCK YOU ! LOOK AT MY FACE. GET THE FUCK OUT NOW.

The commotion from BURNS antics in rage grows louder and with more provoking to call the police persuades them to leave abiding his orders. CUOCO in a far perimeter can be heard with his endless giggling outburst. Until they're exited out with BURNS slamming the door shut behind as it echoing pitched matches BURNS remaining fit.

With them all back in the car in clear distance away from BURNS and his office. Relief of the thought being in handcuffs possibly but damaged severely due to their splitting ties in a unfavorable way they did BURNS on the account of a madman like CUOCO shattering his mouth to something he most deserved. ALEX contemplating out loud of what is their next agenda now that they no longer had a strong attorney representing them, his chances of being in jail or even worst death row bound seem to move closer and closer to likelihood on his behalf.

ERNEST is more fed up with the likes of VIC CUOCO, his presence around them isn't bringing any clues and links to their situation. Something he's paying him hefty to solve, not discharge more turmoil and disaster that flings in their path.

- You know what I'm thinking right now ?

ERNEST says.

- What ?

ALEX replies.

- We need to just start this whole thing over, a clean slate. A new attorney, possibly a bodyguard, and most definitely a new investigator. Anything but hang around this fucking rumble tumble cheap skate because I see where were heading with you. And its a cold box with a steel bar gate in front it. We don't need any of this shit, I tell you what, I'll drop you off at your office, you keep the money, and we go on our way. How do you feel about that ALEX ?

ERNEST cries out in passion towards CUOCO, who's looking on with his eyes real low like he's been double crossed.

- That sound good to me pop. Yea.

ALEX says.

- It's all up to you guys. You wanna ditch me because what I did to that muthafucka back there fine. It's your dollar but guess what ? I didn't sound out that fucker "DOUBLE R" name and address back there for nothing. And if he's involved and signed those letters like you said he did. I can clear bookies from here to Vegas that'll the bet the both of you won't make it in the next few days, I guarantee. I mean...well that is, without my help.

He says.

- How well you know the mother fucker ?

ALEX asks.

- I know him well enough to tell you I've pinched him down three times, and he's the size of a fucking sky scraper. I also got word that he's got more bodies of people on him than Vietnam and yellow fever combined. I picked him up last time on a investigation from a guy who paid me twenty thousand dollars.

He says.

- What for ? I mean what he'd do.

ALEX asks.

- The guy said he was linked to over seven murders with a positive he's done at least four of them, but the guy wasn't completely sure in pinpointing the son of a bitch because he apparently he didn't use firearms. Look I know where his guy lives and drives, a 77' Monte Carlo; green . We can go over there now, wait for him, take him in, show the police the papers and your free. If not and you let me go, there is no guarantee in my mind if that letter have his initials from that guy, it doesn't matter what you did. You two are fucked. It's up to you two... like your father insinuated indirectly. I've been paid.

Getting away from CUOCO was the easy the part the two could imagine. But to revamp a plan in time that could by chance score them victory and pardon for all crimes ALEX is suspected of committing including first degree murder cannot be apart of overcoming any odds. Compared to the position that they're confronted with there inside the car with someone who's most undesired after bearing toleration with a lunatic such as CUOCO in his own conception. So as much as they like to rearrange the situation its almost impossible with the pressure that's weighed against them.

Once CUOCO put their cards on the table in front of them for a more realistic stance, they take him up on his offer again, strictly with backs against the wall even more. ERNEST then asks CUOCO the address and off they are to the place in goal.

No less than a mere twenty minutes later, adjacent to a highway off an avenue tagged as " Eastern" the group find themselves in a area of the district unfamiliar to them in more ways they care speak of out loud but internally swarming in their minds from the way their body movement transitions from relax to jitter isn't hard to convey. This is something more outstanding with ALEX and ERNEST who as the car coast down the open ghetto streets with people in the tons all touched from the sun are in geographic domination from the sidewalks, street crossings, playground blacktops, bus stops, house stoops, and store front gatherings. It's nothing in comparative to CUOCO who looks on from his window barely seeming as he times his look from his passenger seat view. While it differs for the other two and he comes in realization of this strikingly as they come to a light where they're car is boxed in between two other vehicles who's music volume are peaked at the limit. On the right side where CUOCO does his eye wandering in the streets he's finds himself locked in a vision scuffle at sight with a young black youth behind the wheel of an burgundy Lincoln. The young rough who eyes stretch in a squint of fury and violent capability creeps by real slow in acceleration as his music tops the entire space like a stereo would at a block party or picnic. He looks at CUOCO as if he's in a mirror gazing not at him but through him. CUOCO does the same attempting to equalize that he's just as macho at the youth in his street tests. But when the youth ease his window down in fury to respond, CUOCO snaps his head away before he can even spark a word toward him.

The same happens on the opposite side where ERNEST and ALEX direct their attention in seek from the car like an ability they cannot help. It unfolds but with a much more older gentlemen in a regular Chevrolet. He sees the two whites paying too much attentiveness to himself than they should and before he can stare them down. ERNEST whispers to ALEX behind his seat.

- Don't look at him.

Quickly on cue they both snap from his direction and the light burns the color green to push on and they gladly do. ERNEST cramped in comfort switches his car door for locked although they've already been and says.

- I don't like the feeling of this.

He says.

- Me neither, you didn't say we'd be on this side with those...

ALEX agrees.

- Those who ? The niggers, well where the hell you think he'd stayed. In candy land, where all the people were made out of candy canes and gumdrops. They had broads with tits the size of Tonka truck marshmallows. Get the fuck outta here... You jackasses make the fucking ghetto and now scared to walk around it too. Forget about it.

It isn't for long that they arrive at the building. CUOCO points it out for them distinctively with ERNEST slowly accelerating down the street trying his best to stay visual as possible to his directions. And to not make eye contact with anymore road warriors that nearly turned him and ALEX more whiter than a ghost minutes before. They park on the street, a short distance range from the entrance, ERNEST releases the lock hinges for them to depart but CUOCO lends them cautionary recommending as avocation once they get inside the apartment. Schooling them that its best that they stayed close to him in all times. In the middle of his informing he brings out from behind his rear waist line a chrome colt commander in .45 caliber there gripped in his right hand with his index finger in mode around the stiff trigger. It carried a few scratches ERNEST observed on the barrel but it shimmered still as he check the magazine to be full for action once it showed up. CUOCO fools around more with his pistol inspecting his sights then the barrel.

ALEX looks on from the backseat trembled from his nerves staring down at the gun and wondering the worst with it being in the hands of someone like CUOCO, what has he gotten himself into, and perceiving the outcome to be more atrocious than his instincts expectations awards him to be in ahead of time. Right before they get out he asks CUOCO one last question.

- Look you sure you know what your doing ?

CUOCO cringes his face in frustrations to his question and then responds typically in his demeanor.

- Hey, look shut the fuck up alright. I been running down punks and bagging then away since you were cradled in your mommy arms sucking her tit for milk, okay. Now get the fuck outta the car and the both of youse try to do at least one fucking thing for my sake, please ? And that's not get me plugged before my retirement in miami. LETS GO !!!

Pass they go with a triple shut sound of the doors shutting behind them. Up to the main entrance as they cut through the door lingering past one soul, an elder woman on her way out into street. Who can't help but to glimpse a look at all three in the face CUOCO, ALEX, and ERNEST in surprise with all three white males brushing by her there in this neighborhood in a hustle. Up the stairs they follow CUOCO in the lead to the third and final floor. He remembers clear that his apartment number is 303.

- Here it is...

CUOCO says very low.

- What now ?

ERNEST asks.

- Shhh !

He hushes.

CUOCO then describes the two to stand closest away from the door as he goes in to knock, it isn't wise a move when in this neighborhood where for sure everyone strapped at all times. There isn't a answer, he tries for a second time a bit more louder and for the second attempt there still isn't any response.

- You smell something ?

ERNEST utters.

- Yea whatever it is, it stinks to the shit too.

ALEX responds.

CUOCO popping out a credit card from his wallet and proceeds on shoving it deep into the space nearest to the door knob, determined to creep pass the lock in a reckoning force for entry. But once he places his hand on the knob and he turns it a full clockwise for access. Finding that measure doesn't need to be handled, out whips he does with his pistol in his right hand turning the knob open a crack. Booting in he does the door imploding inwardly. The stench they smell has now caught all their senses now that its recognized from coming within the apartment.

Dashing inside carefully shielding his nose with his shirt, checking all perimeters for anyone. Swift and efficient to a patrolman officer. ALEX and ERNEST press through over his shoulder while shutting the door for no surprises. They stand in awe to the room's empty containment and nose covered with their shirts from the bad odor. The apartment space is so snug that no one would have a problem telling if there was any existence around. CUOCO heads in persistence in his cop prototype parading through the home in and out from the kitchen, bathroom, bedroom, even the closets. Other than speckles of water leftover around the bathroom and kitchen sink which signals that their suspect (DOUBLE R) may have been there sometime earlier. There isn't any for sure indication that they're heading somewhere for his capture. In anticipation as to what was the next move. ALEX opens up to CUOCO shouting out from the living room as he inspects deeper into the drawers inside the bedroom.

- Hey CUOCO from the looks, I'm not even sure anyone lives here.

ALEX says. CUOCO with his hands everywhere and anything he can find. Strapped with a bandana over his face that he came across. He sets his sight fondling through a clothes chest while in the bedroom, with ALEX shouting at him he searches and finds a few sacks of pre-packaged marijuana zip locked inside a sandwich bag. " Lucky me " he says whispering softly to himself trying his best not to be detected. He snatches the bags and stuffs them into a sock before shoving them inside his jacket.

- Hey pops ...

He yells out to ERNEST.

- Yea...

ERNEST replies.

- Do me a favor and find some tape.

He asks.

- Tape ? What do you need tape for ?

ERNEST curiously asks.

- To wind over your kid's bitchy mouth... Christ.

He angrily says. ALEX grows weary of CUOCO'S demoralizing remarks toward him and he makes it known between his father.

Concurrently in the bedroom CUOCO with an anxiety steamed in theft, manages to trip himself into yet another goody stash that was propped to be hidden from all eyes particularly those who are light in the hands equivalent to perpetrators like himself. Under a drawer chest coated in dust and a childhood picture framed on top of it. With his snooping he finds having trouble shutting the last drawer case. Behind to his finding there's a box wrapped in rubber bands. He slides the box out of the closed space darkness and it doesn't take seconds after he dissembles the bands with a flip knife from his pocket. Inside there's three cramped rows of large assorted dollars bill tightly ranging from twenty, fifty, and hundred stacked. Seeing the stored treasure at once catapults his spirits into a galaxy surrounded in bliss, beaming there on the floor with eyes you can see the dead presidents reflection from the box now in his vision sight. Looking in unspeakable glory, CUOCO can only say one word from his mouth.

- For me ? Of course I will.

He runs his finger past each bunch, observing each bill to be complete all in one piece. Quickly after, with watching the bedroom door for no interruptions from his compatriots who are steps away. He finds himself a bag and places it inside for his taking.

When he finishes, he comes back to the living room with ERNEST and

ALEX looking at him and curious to what he has in the bag. He steers away from the question to peep from the living room window for an opening to a breath of fresh air.

- Did you at least find where the hell that smell was coming from ?

ALEX asks.

- NO...

CUOCO answers him. Viewing from the window.

- ... Look, now I've checked around and couldn't find anything but the bathroom and kitchen sink have both been ran today.

CUOCO explains.

- So what that means ?

ALEX replies. CUOCO sighs in frustration.

- It means that our company was here but looks to have made a trip.

ERNEST hints.

- That's right so if we stick around here for a little longer we'll definitely increase our chances as to bumping into him and finishing this.

- But we can't sit here with the fucking place smelling this.

ALEX says.

- Do you want to sit here or a jail cell in between a spade and a hillbilly the size of this fucking building. They ain't had no women in a while, but you Richie Rich will do in the moment of urge. Get me ?

CUOCO replies angrily.

- I didn't think so. We wait here for "DOUBLE R" waltz his ass through the door.

CUOCO parks himself to a seat closest to the door with his gun that he mounts up in his hand tempting for letting loose in the deadliest slaying once their man lay claim across the doorstep. ERNEST passes by him to treat himself into the kitchen and helps himself to a bowl from the cabinet then a spoon below in the drawer. Over the refrigerator he spreads the cupboard apart and finds himself his own treasure that's been a new gold for him as of recently and he doesn't mind showing it. Stretching a smile when he grabs the box of Froot Loops from the shelf and mixed them in the bowl with milk. Boosting his enjoyment.

ALEX spreads open the window for fresh air, then he tracks into the bedroom space trailing what his inquiring mind leads him. CUOCO sees and confesses as a heads up for him to watch his step from all the junk around and bad smell. ALEX goes along as if he doesn't take what he says in consideration even though the trashy clutter is present. He looks over at the closet door that's cracked open from littering objects and opens it for a peek. Everything crammed to the floor looks to be tampered and ran through, a easy duty he suspects CUOCO to be related to being that he had first found himself meddling at.

Over at the drawer near the bed. He holds the picture frame up for looking, blowing the dust away from the image intended. The portrait printed is of a little boy being held by his mom in a past time with a fall setting background. ALEX overlooks the frame for some seconds before retiring it to the dresser top where somehow he fidgets wrong and he falls to the floor.

- Damn !

He says. Bending down on one knee, ALEX reaches down to retrieve the captured memory. When its in his hands and he picks it up and then turns it over. There's a wet red stain on the back looking ALEX in the face no different than a stranger, armed with the stink that fills the entire home in disgust. He touches it and faces a unwanted strange sense of familiarity. Like seeing BELLE'S dead face in a tub filled to a bath of her own blood. Down on the floor once again he finds the blood spilled and soaked fresh into the carpet. At the door he looks in suspense while the other attend outside unknown to his frightening discovery. ALEX stoops down real slow and easy where the portrait had fallen and where blood is traced. Appearing there on the carpet like heavy red cough syrup. ALEX sees the tracks not only appearing on top of the carpet but it seems it too traces under the bed. Leading to something that his mind tells him not to bother, but his instincts take over in a intensive way in desire to see.

He tucks his head down covering his nose, the smell is too awful and grows even severe the more he makes his way to view whatever is concealed below the bed. Tracking spills deepened in red blood to it's origin. With his head sunken down to the depths of the mattress, he sees a dark object lying there where it must have come from. With his heart racing and tumbling inside him, ALEX grabs the object tight into a grip and its much more heavy than he expected but he does manage to drag it into the light to get a good look at what he's actually giving hard pulls to. When finished he stands and realizes that's he's been tugging on a extended bag with a huge zipper in the middle like a face and that the unknown object is the root of the suffering scent. He lays in fear glancing at the zipper there in quaking panic, suddenly he acts on impulse and clamps his fingers around the zipper and slowly slides it down its braces with the stench escaping from inside in the worst imagine. ALEX gawking in surprise and his pulse curdling to see what's inside. What he sees turns him upside down in a instant moment once the zipper is down and the object is revealed. He sees the torso of a body with its center cavity split open like a morgue cadaver grotesquely disfigured and even more shocking the head appears to been decapitated roughly at the shoulders. A horrifying sight of all sights to see. The same with the rancid smell.

ALEX shrieks away from it in screams and hollers so abruptly that his father and CUOCO overhears from the other room before instantly dashing inside to see what was the point of his sudden commotion from silence. ERNEST closest to the room sprints in first to see his son fallen to his backside in fright pointing over to a rotten corpse with the head missing with flies beginning to gather to serenade with the terrible decomposing odor. His eyes pierce at the sight staggering a from the floor back unto the wall as his father enters and views the scene in grotesque.

-My god…the fucking things head is missing.

Inches away behind him driven in force of exhilaration is CUOCO. Making matters much worst by not even festering to his brain to see why it is ALEX made himself known through his emergent wailing. When he gets beside the two appalled in viewing what is before them. CUOCO joins in gawking at the disfigurement for seconds until he lifts his .45 in hand and blaze out the barrel sending shots over at it three times simultaneously. Scoring rounds piercing the old thing twice with the last shot missing and splintering through ALEX'S lower leg as he shuffles his limb on the pasty blood speckle carpet, screaming aloud with a bullet lodge in his leg. Panicking to avoid the gunfire when the trigger is pulled unexpectedly. ERNEST on impulse raced to steer him from the way even though the damage had already been done. He had no complaints in voicing it in his state of mad.

- YOU FUCKING ASSHOLE, YOU SHOT ME IN THE LEG.

ALEX shouts in agony.

- WHY ARE YOU SHOOTING A GUN AT BODY WITH NO FUCKING HEAD ATTACH TO IT.

ERNEST adds while cradling his son as he strains in aching torment from the blow.

When CUOCO finishes ringing out in his maniac demeanor, you can hear ALEX cursing and shouting at the top of his lungs first being at the doorstep to insufferable pain as his leg gushes blood from the bullet circulating straight through his leg. Secondary he spends no expense mouthing dozens of profanities at CUOCO. For lashing out idiotically and targeting live rounds at a dead corpse that's incapable of physical movement.

ERNEST as he holds his injured son sweating and panting from the reckless gunshot wound also spews threatening commentary at CUOCO while aiding to ALEX holding him backwards like a clutch from across his chest. CUOCO'S only response to his unthinkable damages is.

- The both of youse re-fucking-lax I thought fucking thing was alive the way you two were jumping like a couple a fucking church girls.

He responds.

- We have to get him to a hospital, we can't stay here now. And people have to had heard the shots.

ERNEST says.

- If we leave you do realize that this maybe our only shot at getting this motherfucka from now on. And then he's on our tail.

CUOCO replies.

- News flash you nitwit, he's already on our ass. Why the fuck you think we're here.

ERNEST says no more words to CUOCO being that his son is injured from a severe gun shot wound. And his leg is telling the story with it bleeding irrefutably all over the floor. ALEX breathes there covered in rescue from his father in and out with shock and anguish colored on his face.

Eventually they struggle him out of the apartment and to the car in direction to the closest hospital for emergency treatment. In route to the hospital, ERNEST and CUOCO constant shout bicker with each other from his stupid reaction that led them to their never ending dilemma.

As ALEX moans and groans in hurt over the yelling. Strangely in the back seat with his blood smeared everywhere and him losing a fair amount of it from the shirt they bandage around his ankle that doesn't strengthening any pressure to stop the bleeding. ALEX with his hands coated in his own blood, feeling and appearing deeply blurred, he grips his hand firm around CUOCO'S jacket. Breathing in out heavily that saliva seeps almost through his teeth and he asks him a question earnestly.

- What the hell you take upstairs ?

Ask ALEX to CUOCO.

- What do you mean ?

He responds nervously. Stretching eyes on both the father and son after answering in a mild panic.

- Upstairs you did, you took something from there. From that closet and it's killing me. Look at me.

ALEX tells him. CUOCO doesn't go for his clear delusional demands and tears his hands from his jacket. In the back seat directly in his vision you can picture outside his window through the glass. Where he gets a double taking moment from a green car he so happily sees trailing on the opposite side of the street. The same green car he recognizes that belongs to " DOUBLE R".

- There it is...

CUOCO says.

- There what it is...

ERNEST replies.

- That's his fucking car, Double R.

CUOCO tells, pointing outside the car.

- Where ?

ERNEST yells behind the steering wheel.

- He just pass in the green one. Stop the fucking car now.

ERNEST hesitates in the middle of traffic before he tells him again. He turns over to the curb flushing on his emergency blinkers while out swings the passenger door. CUOCO steps himself out with motivation to prove his senses to be correct that what he saw was valid. He lends his plans on to ERNEST like he doesn't have much time.

- You going back there by yourself, shouldn't you at least make a call to the police for back up, just in case.

ERNEST says.

- I don't have time for any of that. Besides I know what I'm doing. Look just take him over to the hospital, keep driving there's one not far from here. I'm a head on back down there and settle this. But when you finish you make sure you get back to your house as quickly as possible I'll be calling you shortly from there.

CUOCO replies.

- Alright !

ERNEST says in farewell. When he pulls off from the curb. CUOCO races down the street like a tail back, brushing against looking on pedestrians, cutting through a alley and making his way up the block in record time back towards to the apartment. He first checks the curb space in front of the building then the opposite sides of that street in hopes to spotting the green Monte Carlo. He sees nothing, next he sprints over to the parking lot with the very same itinerary and walks by every single car as fast as he can, and in the middle he finds it. He looks up from the lot, close in range to the car and directs his eyes up to the floor where the very window view from the apartment is.

CUOCO creeps upstairs carefully trying his best to not be detected by anyone being that he very possibly can fit the description giving to the police by watchful neighbors from the disturbance concerning gunfire just minutes before. He sets before the third floor stairs in parallel to the door. Moving in soft easing pass the steps on to the floor platform, brushing in up against the door.

CUOCO creeps upstairs full in combative mode reserved trying his best to not be detected by a soul being that he's a definite description giving to the police by watchful neighbors from the previous disturbance concerning gunfire earlier that he is responsible for. He sets before the third floor stairs in parallel to the door where the awful smell of rot contaminate the air almost as a poison. CUOCO'S eyes peel wide in disbelief he sees the door to the apartment cracked open. Spaced enough to see a edge of that chair he sat in faced to door. Before he decides to move, there in the hall floor he observed speckles of red that appears to be blood. The small trail is only a few drops that bleeds its way into the hall base and a few steps that he sees. It resonates that the blood must've had came from ALEX and his gunshot wound to his leg. Aiding it with a old shirt, it had to have been flowing so bad that a few drops found itself on the ground when they exited the before.

CUOCO unleashes his pistol from his waist line and then proceeds to move in soundless towards the door. He peeps through the crack but holds off to the side doing his best to not display his footsteps below or his silhouette beaming due to the glare of the rooms gap. He waits a moment for his next decision, thinking that the crevice could be a trick installed assisting him into death if indeed someone's on the other side. CUOCO takes a moment and then kicks the door in and rushes for the move in. Looking for any movement in sight in the living room waving around his piece in its fixed sights. Out he calls for "DOUBLE R" by name all throughout the apartment.

- C'MON OUT MOTHERFUCKER. I saw that green bitch down stairs so I know your in here...

There isn't anything. The apartment's carpet is way too dark for his determination in foot tracks when he goes to searching. He reprises his hunt in both the kitchen and bathroom. In the middle of his commode search CUOCO pulls back the shower curtains and gets the odd sense to know he's around. So out he calls once again speaking out in harshness for the suspect to announce his company.

- I TELL YOU WHAT "R" YOU COME OUT FROM YOUR HIDING AND ACROSS MY HEART AND HOPE TO DIE, ON A STACK OF BIBLES, AND A ETERNITY OF HAIL MARY'S. I won't splatter your brains all over your apartment. HOW ABOUT THAT ? Huh, what do you say, it's a deal ?... FINE HAVE IT YOUR WAY MONKEY... (He chuckles).

Trigger happy with his gun in hand a instinct jolts him to turn around with his back faced to the distance living room and the entrance of the bedroom. At a sight that he thinks is seen involving someone creeping past the bedroom in hurried fashion. When he turns he shoots twice BOOM, BOOM out into the living room. Sending slugs into the wall near the window. There's a misty surrounding in gun smoke leftover and when it clears CUOCO steps out of the bathroom looking around in whatever he thought he saw that commanded his impulsive reaction. He pays the holes he's made in the wall no mind and credits them to paranoia. He checks a closet in the hall that's empty that he never did before and then steps into the bedroom. Now he's aware and knows the headless body of ALEX'S discovery is near so he covers his nose from the stink, he moves in slow passing the bed. Creeped out if he's ever to lay eyes on the thing again and right as he does. He hears the door slam "BOOM" goes the living room door. Similar to someone leaving out. This turns CUOCO attention and he runs out the bedroom and to the door where he sees it closed like before. He looks around the living room one more time and then palms his hands around the knob to open. He pokes his head out the door to check the outer perimeter. And sees nothing different, still left in the desertion it was before he came in. He brings his head back into the door and closes it with a weird and touchy feeling, he feels his mind has to be good as they are with them playing the tricks they're using on him in the eerie moment. But when he turns around there's a pitch black pistol in a hand to the unknown with a extension piece attached to the end of the barrel (a silencer). Right there that meets with the center of his forehead and just before he mouths his last words in a distorted terror centered scream. The trigger goes off and the bullet penetrates his skull in a horrifying rupture from the front to the rear of his head. Sending his body to collapse and fidget backwards from the force of the shot into his unexpected death. And his blood covering the entire door behind him viciously in red splatter with chunks and crumbs of his brain as contents in the hideous mixture.

The unidentified executioner than directly after. With CUOCO'S body slumped up against the door, he shoves his departed body to the floor on the side with his foot harshly. Then grabs him by his legs possessing brute power and drags his body to the bathroom leaving behind a pool mess in brains the size of a road. A flick to the switch for light summons on. And the work to shredding his coat and shirt off to his bare chest comes in. From the process the floor begins to coat in blood from the head shot. This unknown assassin then exits from the bathroom momentarily as a need for something so into the bedroom he goes where he finds the headless body near the bed exposed and places it back into the bag where it's zipped back into its place with ease. Tucking it from being seen.

Next this menacing being with even more strength showcasing tosses over the mattress above the dead corpse propped in the body pouch under the bed. He flips it to the reverse side where he digs into a hole that must've had been made by hand and he removes a sword appearing knife that has to be near twenty inches by the handle. The stainless steel blade pokes out in a chrome scheme tooled for madmess. Marching back into the bathroom with it armed in hand, this individual drives the dagger right into CUOCO'S chest. With it piercing his tissue and bone he leaves it there dead center into his flesh like you would a shovel on a cloud of dirt at the point driven to bury.

5.CHAPTER

Deafening men howls in high-pitch tones sweep through a hospital corridor hauntingly for visitors and awaiting patients. The unstopping screams reside in a room with a number cased beside the door in small numerals (202).

Inside the room on his patient bed, is ALEX who's hollers at the top of his lungs while a surgeon pulls the bullet CUOCO lodged in him out of his own simplicity from his lower leg without any anesthetics on account to the particular hospital not possessing the sedative on behalf of the government issuing statements explaining they don't have the proper funds to itemize it. When in fact they don't intend on providing a mass stock on bulk as other institutions of health, specifically in those hospitals on demographical reasons.

They remove the bullet from his leg, after ALEX endures his extreme amount of excruciating pain and it sets in on him. The doctors bandage his leg in tightly fitted gauges in endless strands. When the grueling procedure entrenched with strain has ended. He's sent on his way standing on two wooden crutches stuffed distressfully under the pit of his arm. Pitifully guided by his dad and a saint nurse into the vehicle for the ride home and rest.

Arriving through the door and with DAISY in uneasiness having been phoning regularly around everywhere possible for their whereabouts and even considering the thought that her two special men may have met their demise, and her only fateful destine next was the dreadful message at her doorstep by two blues in uniform, leaving her weeping in tears when forwarded the news. So they spring into their story on what occurred previously in the day when meeting CUOCO, the scuff at BURNS office departing his representation for them, and how things led to ALEX nearly having his leg taken off by a solid grain caliber cartridge. ALEX informs first, then ERNEST takes seconds after he raids the kitchen for his leftover favorites. Chomping down on his red apple as in the middle to his day reciting.

As they all crowd around into the living room with the television gleaming routine programs. Once their troubles of the day are bestowed upon DAISY in passionate speech. She reacts over the top when its concluded by ERNEST that she put a few clothes in a suitcase and spend a few days at her sister's in Virginia with all that's going on. And can get much more alarming for as long as they're associated with

CUOCO.

- I do not like this, why should I leave here and leave the both of you. My pressure today was through the roof. Do you know what will happened to me while I'm at my sisters and you two are here faced in this catastrophe. My heart would jumped out of my chest and dance on the floor right in front of me.

DAISY says.

- I don't give a damn what your heart does, so long as your ass isn't here. In this house, or in this district. What is going on right now is above supernatural and just seems to get more and more deranged. If there is a god I'd feel he was cursing us for the last days ... and for what I do not know.

ERNEST demands.

- So what you think dad ?

ALEX asks.

- To think, we have no time. To do...we first have to get your mother from here with all that's happen with this son of a bitch CUOCO there isn't no telling what can happen in anytime or moment. As crazy as this motherfucker is we don't have to worry about this spade catching us. He'll kills us for sure.

ERNEST speaks.

- When is the last time you've talked to him ? Did you call his office while at the hospital.

ALEX asks.

- No...but that's a damn good idea.

ERNEST snatches the phone and holds it to his ear with one hand, pressing firm on the numbers as he dials to CUOCO's office with the other. It rings like it's suppose and through the living area ERNEST chews on his apple pacing back and forth in front of the television with all eyes on him. Waiting in expectation for the sadistic likes to answer in his no good delivery. But instead it swaps over to a voice mail. He tries a secondary number CUOCO supplied but found no luck with that one as well. ERNEST tries several more times for the office number when in coincidental CUOCO'S commercial airs on the box there in room, in front of all of them.

- There he goes there...

ERNEST sees while still getting ringing tones on the opposite end.

- You two hired VIC CUOCO the crummy private investigator from the commercial.

DAISY says.

- Believe me we know...

ALEX replies.

- You should call into the closest police station where you left him. I mean if this idiot is as crazy as you say. It's not hard to think he's in custody by now.

DAISY says. Quick ERNEST pulls from the yellow pages from a drawer and calls three precincts in the fifth with no luck, they didn't have any bookings under the last name CUOCO. It isn't until he remembers the address and phones the sixth precincts for his search. When he calls, he gets a response with a officer he complies with his interest easily.

• Hello officer. I'm calling to see if a friend of mines by chance got hauled in this afternoon. I got a bad feeling he's done something I made him promise me he wouldn't do.

• Please hold sir, while I check the booking list. What's his last name ?

• CUOCO !

• Ok, hold please...

• Will do...

The cop places ERNEST on hold. In burst the nightly news wavering on the front screen with the volume elevated by DAISY with the remote. The reporters call for a breaking news in a apparent murder discovery. ERNEST along with the rest tunes in, still with his ear pressed to the phone standing without move from the impulsive moment.

According to the news " A man's body was found on a run path near a park a couple hours ago before the sun went down. The grizzly discovery was too much for the finder to bear. On a ride home from work, the local jogger decided to catch a few laps before accompanying his wife at dinner. He frequents the park all the time because the view, but he didn't expect the view on this day. The jogger stated on his first lap around the park he stumbled his eyes across a heavy large black trash bag. Which seemed to contain something strange and oddly structured from the far appearance. There was a image that came from bag that controlled his attention to it from the forest silence. As he lapped around the park once and then twice he continues to configure what's is this object in this bag from a far. So on his third and last lap, finally he courage's himself to drift over to the object that was planted near a bush off path. As he moves in closer he describes a quaking feeling from his foot, to his spine, then to his brain. The spark had to have came from what he saw next in his finding that was enough to bring anyone to a frantic state in rumbling fear. The jogger came a across a dead human body lying there in complete nakedness with its chest torn open to the rib cage, the sight was a blinding eye to see . He also added that the person who was identified as a male was half covered from the large trash bag as if someone could care less about a individual finding him in place."

" The authorities are hinting to the casualty may have missing organs and the news wastes no time in disclosing identity of the victim as was well known local detective VICTOR CUOCO. Jaw-dropping watching in a circle. ALEX looks on as if he could leap from himself in spirit sitting in disbelief to the reports and findings, corresponding in the dirtiest of words right before his mother as his hard expression to astonishment.

ERNEST'S mouth seeps open as he drops his apple core he was finishing to the carpet floor. Bewildered just as his son to the reports, plugged to the nightly news addressing like it's message is competence. There's only one statement he utters to himself spacing off to the story beholding to them all.

- He got him.

ERNEST says to himself.

Cringing on the couch, sinking his nails deeply into a pillow while his imagination sets in on him as to being next in the slaughter. ALEX continues to look on at the breaking broadcast. ERNEST stands with the phone remaining propped to his ear and on comes the officer back to respond to his adamant question on CUOCO'S whereabouts. Only this cop has disbanded his previous courteous demeanor in assisting to his simple question upon calling. He's now resided from being the answered and now the answerer all of the sudden.

ERNEST still standing with his eyes stretched in awe, appearing disconnected to reality. Hangs into the conversation.

• Hello...

• Yes

• Yes sir, beg my pardon for my long duration in having you wait. But I found something very interesting and I hoping you could explain to me about this CUOCO character. First off, what is your first and last name sir and then may I please have your relation to the prisoner.

ERNEST disconnects the call and steps back to place it back on to the hook slowly. Abandoning the conversation with the officer right away. When he finishes he steps back into the living room where ALEX advises that they contact the police as soon as possible without them going on and taking this dangerous matter in their own hands any longer.

- We have to go to the police ?

ALEX presumes.

- ERNEST, you need to right now. Holding out any longer gives them even more a excuse to finger the two of you for his murder. Even with alibis.

DAISY says.

- Yea that's if we're even lucky to be tried as murder's. If we're even lucky by some chance to see the end of the week. He killed ANNABELLE, you saw the body missing its head under the bed back at the apartment, and now CUOCO the only person who was crazy enough to kill him. If we stick around here without any police notification we're dead dad... I have to call CLARISSA and kids to see if they're unharmed.

ALEX says. Hopping on his injured leg with a single crutch in pursuit of the phone on the counter.

ERNEST remains opposing to any of their wanted suggestions.

- We're not going to any cops.

ERNEST says.

- CUOCO'S is dead dad and now they might think we did it. We have and can prove for a fact who killed him and where he lives. If we don't make any smart moves now we're prolonging our suspected guilt with the police and hurrying through our paths in being next on this psycho's shit list.

ALEX states.

- There is no prolonging what were already held accountable for son.

ERNEST replies.

- Oh my god !

DAISY cries. Raising the volume of the television that directs ALEX attention to the screen where the screen summons pictures of perfect drawn descriptions of his self and his father. With the news reporters voice dubbed over the depictions. They place a ten thousand dollar award for anyone if they're capable of providing any information or intel about them.

- We have to run ?

ALEX demands drastically.

- No, we're going to handle this and set you free then clear our names of all this shit. But first I want your mother out of here... NOOOW I SAID!

ERNEST says. Shouting in mild rage that snaps her from her stubbornness and into abiding his exactions.

- And second ?

ALEX questions.

- Tell me you still have the card I gave you at the hospital.

From his wallet he pulls from the rear in his pants, then flips it open. He pulls the card with the marker name on the front like before, and ALEX places it in his father's hand where he reads the tag blazed in professional text across the card. Clinging it in his fingers reading without moving his lips" MOISSON SERVICES" and the number there at bottom. With his eyes fixed to the card in his hand, ERNEST invests one more thought for one more phone call.

DAISY has her bags packed, ERNEST lugs them to the trunk where she hugs and kisses ALEX balanced on his crutches before she's off. ERNEST advises her to don't stop until she's reached her sisters in Virginia. Once they've settled the ordeal in a day or two she'd be back home and everything will be back to normal in no time. They embrace for a kiss and she starts the engine pulling from the drive away leaving them to execute this risky mission that can lead to more horror or for they're sake a strike in luck that prevails.

The next morning ALEX back into familiarity of his father's old friend MOSS, owner to MOISSON SERVICES. The very same MOSS on strict orders from his father ALEX was to see for a certain confidential job, a year earlier while he laid on his death bed. ERNEST pained in desperation wastes no time in bringing his friend in on him and his son's oppressive pressure they both are faced with in their dilemma, and being at serious risk to being another casualty at the hands of a hellish psycho. Who for most certain have them in his radar for a unknown murderous pleasure that still remains mystery. Their current visit suddenly is in hopes that MOSS could provide one more favor at this more crucial time than ever as time they may not have as each hour passes by.

- So according to your story. Your asserting that your son is being accused to the murder of his girlfriend, then the both of you are also prime suspects in another murder with the t.v jerk detective CUOCO. And that the real person who's responsible for the two poor soul's death is now after you for a reasoning that escapes the two of you for any clues whatsoever.

MOSS says.

- Correct !

ERNEST complies.

- And who is this person, where he lives, what's his name ?

MOSS asks.

- From what we were told and I can verify his name is RONALD RAZOR, he has an apartment off Jay Street in northeast, he lives on the third floor. He also goes by the nicknames " D.R", "DOUBLE R", or sometimes just " RAZOR". I guess I shouldn't have to tell you how lethal he is after me showing up here, do I ?

ERNEST informs.

As he tells, MOSS jots down on his write pad the specifics in front of him on his desk. When he finishes MOSS finds himself reminiscing over the last name RAZOR.

- Hmmm... RAZOR.

He says.

- What is it ?

ALEX asks.

- No I just heard of that name before. RAZOR...

MOSS replies.

- Where ?

ALEX asks.

- I can't remember, so it must isn't too important. I have all I need, so please do me and most importantly yourselves a favor now and do not waste anymore stress regarding this ordeal. Why? Because you came to the right friend, a friend who by my word you can rest to sure that this situation will be very taken care of as quickly as possible...

From his desk he calls outside his office for a secretary with one touch from his phone. When they enter he swipes the sheet he wrote on from the metal binders of the pad, folds it and then hands it off like a note. While its removed out the room by his aid.

- ...you still may have to meet your crisis in court, but you won't have to worry about the dangers when looking over your shoulder once you exit out the oasis of MOISSON SERVICES any further, you can rest to sure on that.

MOSS says.

- Damn that's good to hear MOSS, I swear I don't know what would I do without a friend like you.

ERNEST quotes in sighing relief.

- Well you wouldn't ...

MOSS answers in a bold firm.

- Say again !

ERNEST requests as if he didn't catch what was said.

- Without a friend like me you wouldn't. See if I wouldn't be here, nor would my business. And people like you in the thousands who walk through those doors day in and day out. Explaining and pleading with me and my consultants about yourselves being in unfortunate binds with deadly jokers that puts you on a first class passport to the dooms day. Pardon my expression but if I was to guess, and that guess was the best guess of all my estimates it would be people like you would be found somewhere and god only hopes your all in one piece as your mutilated, soulless flesh sit there in a ditch left into the insane imagination of one sick and twisted motherfucker.

ERNEST and ALEX looks on listening and watching MOSS frightening delivery switch from normal to terror driven at the climax of his speech. Leaving them tensioned internally out of controllably in fear. But he breaks that fear after seeing their scared reaction and bursts out in laughter. Pointing at their poor faces that took his interpreted joke to a more real statement. As he laughs, they grow more comfortable to the so called joke although this instance that involves them they feel doesn't involve any humor whatsoever.

- Now that the nasty is out of the way. It's time for some fun.

MOSS says.

- Fun for you or us.

ALEX asks.

- We'll see it as this. It's fun for you paying and fun for me receiving.

(MOSS laughs more)

Now that they've completed their handling with the likes of MOSS and his shadowed business of associates with promises in a guarantee termination indefinitely and immediately for a ongoing havoc trailing their coat tails. The father and son find rest in a haven of a small but suitable grade. A hotel room at the convenience for safety once the fearful conflict they're faced with has been resolved. All at the complementary expense for sanctuary from MOSS and his associate services who are a approximate basic neighbor near the five star board across the street. A nerved ALEX and his at ease father ERNEST stay put to the room until notification has sent from a direct source.

ALEX in the bed space in front of the equipped television finds himself contemplating thoughts in all directions that display his agitation and spooked fit for what he's had to deal with for a going three days in a private, condemned hell, being recorded like a film in a hamster maze. But what he ponders more on in thought is the mystery of who is MOSS and what exactly his business mobilizes as a service to certain people at only a specific stature. Meanwhile his father in opposite to his displeased emotions carry on near the window view that sets upon across the street where you can clearly see M.S (MOISSON SERVICES) scheming that their trouble is one with the past, you can hear his free tone as he carries on a conversation with DAISY over the phone as she is in close reach to her sisters calling from a gas station pay phone. ERNEST covers indirectly their plight evolving better, as he munches a bowl of FROOT LOOPS in the middle.

- Don't worry... in a day or two, maybe three. Things will be just as before. You call me on this number as soon as you make it to your sister's.

ERNEST says, steady crunchy and slurping away over the phone.

- I will, there was heavy traffic coming in. So I clocked myself, I could be there in thirty to forty minutes. I'll call you then.

DAISY replies. Standing in old telephone post surrounded in rusted metal that coincided with the scuffed glass casing. In between the crosses of a gas station and highway.

- Alright...don't worry and I love you.

He says.

- I will, love you too. Tell ALEX the same for me.

She asks before leaving the call.

- I will, bye.

ERNEST places the phone back on its base and slurps down the remainder of his cereal, finishing with a tasteless burp to wash it down.

- Your mom says she loves you.

ERNEST tells ALEX seated on the bed. He disregards his moms message, and he responds back dead on off subject almost like he's been awaiting the opportunity to.

- Dad, what does MOSS do ?

He asks.

- What do you mean ?

ERNEST replies.

- I mean his business. MOISSON SERVICES, what business does MOSS service to certain people.

ALEX buzzed in curiosity.

- Well, well... I'll put it like this. Certain services in this world son needs to be organize correctly and discretely in catering to what we as particular desired to be done, when we need them to be.

He states trying his best to not reveal anything direct involving the originality of the question.

- So what they kill people to get their point across at the "say so" powers to people like us. Because if it is I can't go on knowing I was apart of something like this.

ALEX speaks in fright and discuss.

- IT'S THE JOB...

ERNEST shouts so loudly that it mutes ALEX.

- It's the job, they provide a service for a business that compensates them. Nothing more, do you understand ?

ERNEST says harsh and direct.

- However they do that service isn't any business for us to know. It's done, over, we move on. We have way more serious things to reflect on like your freedom than to feel a way for some nigger who you know and I know got everything coming to him. Do you understand, does that answer your question ?

ERNEST finalizes strongly.

- Yea...

ALEX replies clearly unsatisfied.

- Now hand me the remote, it's Lakers night.

Upon speaking to her husband minutes after. Still placed at the gas station off the highway. DAISY purchases some treats from the inside store, then helps her way back to her car. In sure of her destination reach to her sisters in no time. As she exits the station store, at one of the regular pumps sits a car and a gentlemen from the looks fueling it for ride. She pays no attention to the person, despite the two only being the rest stop's only moment customers. DAISY finds herself to the car, hops in after a shuffle with the key that pops opens the driver's side. And she starts the ignition switch, flooring life to the automobile, coasting off in pursuit easy slow to the highway intersection. But as she's moving, there's a feeling, the car isn't moving as it should and there's definitely a problem now that its beginning to wobble in stagnation towards the front of the vehicle. She doesn't even make it to the tip of the entrance way for her exit, when she yields in park, and ejects her door in observation to the problem.

- What the hell ?

She says in small talk out of frustration to herself.

With the engine still flowing nice and quiet and her headlights in full glow. She turns to the front of the car peddling over noisy rocks that floor the ground from footsteps for inspection and then to the side. She looks down at the tires, from her looking point in the darkness they seem a bit off but indecisive from lack of light. DAISY bends down and runs her hand over and against the grooves of the tires, they feel off too. Hopefully it isn't deflated comes to her mind. Quickly from the trunk she grabs a handy flashlight and then flickers it on to verify the problem, and like her first instinct when the light beams on the tire, she finds the driver's side down. Which explains the rocky motion as she made her attempt off after starting. Pondering on what to do next, she lifts the trunk ajar and removes a list of needed for her objective. Primarily the spare tire hidden deep below the depths, then the jack and rod for elevation off the ground. After helplessly establishing her willed strength toting the spare on her own over to the passenger's side where the deflated wheel is, all DAISY'S courage in the world doesn't conceal her womanliness. So while stooped down matching herself loosen the no good tire's nuts with the jack rod, and a flashlight for proper view. Steps from ordinary sneaker shoes arise on the rocks near her space coming from around the car to beside her, appearing to belong to a gentlemen who's knee sit adjacent to DAISY as she recognizes his presence upcoming and she ceases her work and turns to this figure with sincerity and kindness in his tone of voice.

- Excuse me ma'am, but can I lend you some assistance.

Daisy looking paused at the man first, then after he issues his help that holds her to affection that he's candid in favor. A smile waves over her face as having met contact with relief.

Meanwhile back at the hotel, ERNEST and ALEX tuned intuitively to a ongoing Laker game that blasts in exceeding boisterous volume, almost as if your really in the surroundings of a ball game from the audience seats. Capturing the true to life, gameplay experience at every referee's blow of the whistle. ALEX with his feet propped in ample state at the television. While ERNEST does the same in the deep middle of a red apple like always. Following every move the highlight sensation Earvin "Magic" Johnson does as he ascends the ball beautifully from the backcourt for a spectacular score in televised color. It isn't much seconds later when the hotel phone rings and its answered by ALEX who signals his father still eyes forward at the game, that its for him. He removes from the seat and picks up the phone from his side of the room and he finds it to be MOSS behind the call, ERNEST immediately sense problems.

- Yea...

- It's MOSS...

- Is everything in place, are we ok ?

ERNEST says, speaking in a mutual code.

- No, I called because I want to follow up on some of those details you gave me earlier.

- What is it ?

Sensing by his tone there's something troubling.

- I need to know do you know anything else on this RONALD RAZOR, anything exact in detail.

- The only thing I know from what my attorney told me was he's a real nut case. CUOCO took the time out before he showed up dead, that we were in for something with this fucked

He detailed.

ALEX looks over at his dad in immediate panic, anticipating problems that comes from the messenger from the other side on the phone.

- Yea well he didn't lie, some workers of mine found a headless body from the feet to torso under his bed at his apartment and it stunk worst than garbage.

- You found it...we saw it there too.

- I made some phone calls before calling you, according to his only living relative, a cousin. Turns out according to her, RAZOR'S been missing for almost five months. It hasn't been any sign of him, no calls or personal contact whatsoever. So that leaves me with gut intuition on this one.

- Draw your conclusions.

- Well I know he's a wanted man and he can't be around here as hot as he is without being hauled in at some point. Other than the foul smell in his apartment, no one in his building or in the street has came in contact with him which tells his cousin story to be true. So either he did get missing, or that's RAZOR'S body rotting under that bed.

Bell tone sounds the floor as doors to the level floor elevator surface wide to an apparent figure that steps off. Tracing his movement beyond the suspended service. Appearing as a male goes the being steady in pace carrying a package in both hands as it stretches before his chest as he moves normal in his stride. Lapping past every door on the floor until arrival shows to the one he intends for delivery.

- Are you telling me what I think your saying.

- Depends…if your saying the buck you had all along was your stalking maniac, your wrong. But if you was thinking after I just told you that someone played you two like a fiddle, well I'm afraid so old friend.

In the strange shift into the conversation, a solid knock at the door is heard. In repeated knocks regular. " Tap, tap, tap, tap" instantly everything becomes quiet in a snap of a finger, the only noise comes from the television which proceeds on still louder. When they lock eyes on one another in a unwanted surprise filled in extreme tension, worried the sicko has finally found his way to them to collect a debt with their lives. ERNEST moves closer to the door, lifting his finger to his lips at ALEX to remain silent and still has his ear glued to the phone, mumbling from MOSS on the other side of the phone before he's hushed also. ALEX shuts down the volume at the t.v. ERNEST next staring anxiously from the inner peep hole to the one that sits out. Hoping to catch a look at whomever it is knocking at the door continually.

He sets his eyes through the hole and sees a figure but not a face to the identity that's relevant to his recollection. ERNEST has had enough of the knocking when he swings open the door likes he's catching whoever on the other side in a act that shouldn't be spoken on. Standing there knocking the whole time entirely is no man preconceived to them as to being a slave to determined retribution at all. Only a average old messenger deliverer, armed with no vengeance sought upon or weapon. But a regular uniform with a package occupying the freedom of his hands. It's apparent they've reached new stakes in fear from one man and they realize it. The only simple thing to do is to accept their package with little dignity they have left. Just before they do the deliverer asks a few simple questions routine in dropping off shipments.

- ALEX ST.CLAIR is that you sir.

The deliverer states.

- That's my son...

ALEX still in place by the bed looking on.

- I have a package here for him.

- From whom ?

ERNEST asks.

- Uh...the sender and name is on the label tag. Sign here for me please.

The deliverer extends a clipboard with paperwork for the item. Requesting a signature from ERNEST who provides before heading off.

- Thank you, good evening.

He shuts the door and glimpses down at the label wording encasing on the package. The name in capital lettering "MOISSON SERVICES" with "H. MOSS" (his birth name) above the address. He hands it off to ALEX.

- It's for you.

- What is it ?

Scraping the tape sealed edges from the box, uncertain and desirable at the same time to know what's in stored for him. ERNEST motions over to the corner returning to his call with MOSS.

- What happened, what was that ?

- Oh it wasn't nothing, why didn't you tell me you sent a package...

All the while after discarding the box wrappings. ALEX finds enclosed inside, two items, a folded letter, and another item that remains unknown with it being decorated in Christmas paper, a gift within a gift to some sort.

ERNEST carries on regularly. While MOSS gets specific on a package he's unknowing that was sent to ALEX by him.

- Package ? What package your talking about ?

- The package you sent to ALEX by the messenger a minute ago. Your name and company was on the senders address.

ALEX unfolds the letter and goes in on reading its message.

" We're almost there, with everyone else out the way. It's just you and me now. Read the numbers and then enjoy the view to the right."

Momentum rising through ALEX in a alarm phase as he grabs the second item inside the box with above caution. He slowly in scare with his palms sweating, he removes the gift paper and finds himself a tiny deck of cards. He reads the first one with a huge print of the number five on it in red marker. Then slides over to the next while placing the last card in the back of the deck. There's another card that reveals another card with another number in the same red marker and this time its the number four. Then three... ALEX reaches a state in shock of unsure was about to take place. He yells out to his father, "Dad...dad... dad" still in confusion with MOSS about the validity of it deriving from him or not.

- ERNEST why the hell would I send a package to your son or even you for that matter. When I'm across the street, wouldn't it be more simpler for me to pass whatever it is I have to tell you over the phone.

What MOSS explains sits in his acceptance. ERNEST then turns around to ALEX who's calling him and his son's look, says more than what needs to be said as he stands there holding cards in his hands. It charges him over the room to see the explanation to his son's cries. When he does and notices the number one in bold red marker ink blazing from the front of card that lay in his hands with the others in count down fashion behind it. He doesn't understand and so he asks.

- What the hell is this ?

ALEX doesn't reply in answer as he turns that card away under the deck to reveal one last card that sits in the deck, only this one isn't labeled or flashing large numerals in fire red colors. It's an arrow pointing in the right direction outside, which is across the street to MOISSON SERVICES. Still with his face stuck to the phone and the only sound from it comes from the opposite end where MOSS in repeat dialogue asking over "Hello, hello, hello". When ERNEST and ALEX on intuition follow the direction off the card in front of the two of them, they hear it, they see it, and it happens... BOOM.

6.CHAPTER

Towers of glass shattering inwardly into their room eruption from impact, power outages circulate actively and without question in the entire hotel. Everything turns pitch black. Deaf tone from the BOOM rumbles in the air distortedly. Off their knees from the eruption that gave a flash into the present once Armageddon shows. Hobbling without any clear hearing for seconds, once they reach their feet and inspect that they're alright and aren't missing anything from wallet to limbs. All but tiny spectacles and particles lodged in face and arm skin with blood trickling down from the hurtful wounds. They console with each others safety, blurred almost. In more than confusion to what just took place. They interact the first time in the aftermath, unknown to the cause or where it even came.

- What the fuck just happened ?

ERNEST clinching his hand around his neck in agony whirling his head from the impact sets his vision across the room to something breathtaking as ALEX speaks. From the bulging in his eyes sprouting in colossal whatever imagery mystifying enough to command his attention encourages him to point his finger across the room. ALEX views his recognition and before he knows his face is astounded no different than his father when he sees the window blown in complete. No curtains, no metal liners, and all the glass that compensated once before the glorious view gone, all gone.

- Whatever it was blew the glass from windows.

ALEX in lead moving unbalanced into the clearing opening that before instilled a window seal, trampling over scattered pieces of glass molding to the soles of their shoes in each pace with ERNEST directly behind. Outside in the streets and inside the hotel hallways you can empathize distantly the painful cries in misery mixed with panic and never ending alarm trips buzzing in and out. Overlooking the external carnage committed. ALEX hawks down still mentally phased and disoriented into the smoky wind spotting around to recollect memory in the area perimeter after the incident. This doesn't prolong when in seconds he realizes in death struck. The occupying space where MOISSON SERVICES was minutes before across the way unharmed is demolished, destroyed, devoured, consumed in destruction. ALEX points from their floor to the leftovers that resemble a crumbled snowman constructed in pure coal, in the finishing process as emblems of flames still burn around it.

Leaving from the room ambitious to the outside. Into the flustered hallways where there's countless mobs of people evacuating from the building with voices embedded in depression snapping from every direction. The elevators are down while the panic and fire alarm blare disturbingly in alert throughout the floors and entire building encouraging the immediate exits. Maintaining to stay close ALEX and ERNEST take the stairs with hundreds of other frightened visitors and guest. All in uncomfortable navigation to the lobby floor. Upon arrival they find even more bunches of individuals crowding the lobby area. Careless to find whether or not the body of people are exiting or stilled. ALEX and his father finesse themselves passed everyone to gain reach to the outside. When they do, a chilling finding they come across that had to spawn regretful thinking in choosing their exit strategy.

Before passing the doors, a consoling employee of the hotels hold everyone's attention in leaving from the building and into the streets at their own risk ahead of the police and paramedics accession. He isn't clear in description to his advisory but he does stay firm in his indirect recommendation when using statements such as " I advocate for everyone to stay inside until the authorities and paramedic arrive"; "Please people do consider the thought at exiting at this time."; "If you plan on leaving, do at your own risk".

The hirelings discouragements are withstood by the majority even with the lobby floor overcrowding more and more. But with those who are unwilling and budge to his forewarn cast themselves out in the decaying scene. In their deepest regret to not abide by the worker's alerting disapprove they see first hand. Shoving the concerned staff member from out of the way with many more in like minds as himself in their determined direction is ALEX. He doesn't pay any mind as the worker remain in samaritan mode as he attempts to palm his hand in a clinch around ALEX while whispering with all eyes of visitors on him nearly begging for him to not step foot outside there. "Sir, please for your own good, DO NOT GO OUTSIDE THIS DOOR". It isn't effective though, ALEX moves along in continuing to push him aside without saying word and his eyes straight ahead mirroring himself external through the entrance double glass doors as the followers behind him do the same when they reach the outer oasis.

Feeling that there can't be anything worst than a few destroyed buildings that he viewed from his window range. Wrong in his thinking. Once outside with his father and others all close by in their sight, the damage is completely different than what was seen from upstairs, the damage is more surreal in the capacity to cataclysmic. Seeing the leftover hold in comparisons to ground zero, in a horrible trance looking around into the cloudy smug of smoke as littering trash and building cement fills everywhere. Reflexes from instant coughing arise from almost everyone as they move out, staring glances at the madness hovers around them like a nuclear bomb had met on this one square block alone. Folks eyeballing cars totaled upside down or torn in half, neighboring buildings with charred sections in need of renovated repair, the hotel's outer which was in luxury before, now leaning towards a ghetto-project rundown appeal now that almost every window had been blown in. From the explosion, and then the building that rested MOISSON SERVICES bound with even more unlucky than the others with it somehow failing to resemble an appearance of ever being a concept. It's shattering garners a somewhat respect to the level of explosives used to bring it to pieces.

Not a minute goes by and a few steps from the door past when suddenly like a wave shock. A womanly shriek rings out to the far left, quick ALEX, ERNEST, and others curve to the attention of a woman amongst them who continues her screaming as she backs herself away in steady motion pointing then shouting hysterically "THERE'S SOMEONE ARM RIGHT THERE". They all grasp at the sight for confirmation to her claim, that wasn't near a fib or a case of mistaking an object. Everyone brace themselves to see something so bizarre and freakishly out of place in their imagination as the disfigured limb lie there on the ground deformed. Abnormal to see a severed forearm on the ground like a piece of trash, mind questions aren't even able to surface when another person such as the women pinpoints another discovery. This time a man points out a body up ahead in the street faced down like its face is buried in the road pavement. As much as everyone wants to turn and look away they set their sights and try to look real close, once again a confirmation to if it is what the individual claims. Indeed its a lifeless body stretched out. At that moment things turn into game of death, how others begin to spot more bodies lying around the entire block perimeter. You can hear more shrieks from the first woman and many more from the others. "OH MY GOD", "I THINK IM GOING TO BE SICK", "WHO ON EARTH WOULD DO SOMETHING LIKE THIS".

ALEX looks over at his father after the comments are made aloud insinuating through look his awareness of who's responsible. They all decide to retreat back into the hotel lobby, haunted by what they've seen. A clear recognition as to why the employee was avid about no one exiting in the first place. As someone knocks on the door and its met with workers who demandingly invite them back inside away from the horror site. Lagging behind the group as they all head back in one at a time. ALEX feels a drop to his head, assuming it could be rain, but when the minor fluid spills again and then more. His natural reaction is to wipe it from his head with his hand. So when he does he looks down at it judging it to be water when in fact it isn't. The pasty thick drops are blood, when instantaneously ALEX stops in his tracks to look above at where a huge plated glass platform is modeled to deter messy weather from incoming and registered guest.

On cue when whatever inside strengthens him to look up just in time. From above he finds the sky clamoring in full collapse. Fast on thinking ALEX pushes his father the person in front of him who's last to enter inside the hotel. Escaping from its deadly air boundaries sending the sizable piece straight down to the sidewalk breaking it to million of pieces. But it doesn't stop there, the giving reason for the platform falling in the first place is due to it carrying a body on top after the explosion. The weight of the crisped corpse had to been so great, it left the platform no choice but to stagger and fall. And when it does with great disgust when it comes from thirty- five, or forty feet in the air and hits the ground at that very moment like a tomato. A packet of blood bursts all over them in a dreadful impact. The bystanders scream out frantically after being doused in the red bodily gore. ALEX catches the most of it with the blood ricocheting his face in a grisly fashion being that he was closest to the base entrance. Paused from moving or even getting to his feet, ALEX halts there on the ground frozen stiff to the bone, breathing in and out with a face painted in blood. The way he moves speaks to his exhaustion in this relentless chase that he can't quite comprehended to whether this maniac intends to wipe him out or anguish him intensely. Perhaps it isn't one or the other but both, either way he has no answer. No answer why is this happening to him, no answer who's actually doing it, and no answer in how to fix it now that there's no MOSS or no more MOISSON SERVICES left standing. Leaving the only open option to put into action after seeing the extremity of how far this killer's willing to go by detonating bombs to destroy buildings with hundreds of innocent civilians circle amongst.

Away from the hideous havoc at the hotel and the massacre left behind that claimed dozens of bodies on the account and expense of them. The thought of the trail of gurneys that follows one after another. Not also counting the deaths of ANNABELLE, CUOCO, AND MOSS. Who were personal subjects snuffed away on behalf's never to be scene again but their deaths longed etched into each identities like memory. This killer putting to rest this cat and mouse race and finishing both of them will do a greater good if the law doesn't first.

Racing past the home door and slamming it shut as assuredly locked for no surprises, ALEX with his father ERNEST clear every drawer in reach stuffing every piece of belonging that is wanted in each of their briefcases hurrying as their lives depend on it and it does in the front of each of their minds they know every minute a bit slower makes this maniac more closer and closer. At their speed looking on its synonymous to a team swapping tires at a car grand prix. In abroad throughout the house at the top of his lungs from the other room. ALEX hears his father count out to him, to be prepared in the next five minutes for their departure and don't be forgetful in swiping his passport. At Reagan National there's two tickets for the thirteenth row all aboard a flight to California with their names on it. The city of angels in choosing precisely because if there's any more running to be made it could be pointed to the boarder. ERNEST ceases in packing any more personal items, he doesn't even hesitate to rundown a check for everything he has. He swipes a portrait of him and DAISY next to the lamp, peeps for a second and then shoves it into his bag before flipping the switch and leaving his room pitched in darkness. Down the stairs he goes, dropping his things to the front of the door and then proceeds to peep through the peephole and then outside the nearest window to the door. Clearly shaking with paranoia, he considers in opening the door but pauses himself, takes a few steps back with his head crooked in a form that can attribute to him thinking. He acts next by stepping over to the nearby closet and reaches over some old clothes in the darkness toward the upper shelf compartment and he removes a regular shoe box enclosed with a .44 special buried in a spill of bullets.

He snaps open the empty chamber and loads up. When its ready he goes back to door, from up the stairs comes ALEX.

- You ready ?

ERNEST asks.

- Yea...how about you ?

He shoots back.

- Let's get outta here.

When his father gets more closer, ALEX gets a good look at the gun he has in his right hand wrapped around, doing his best to keep out of his sight while he shields his leg.

- Think we have the time to use that now.

ALEX alludes.

- Doesn't matter, it's only a precaution in case whomever intends to commandeer this evacuation.

He doesn't get the chance to pronounce the remainder of the word from his lips when in the instance the phone there in the kitchen not far from them in a few steps rings. Everything stops within them from movement and thought, their eyes stare at each other in nervousness then it wonders over in the distance to the phone as it rings behind rings. Covering the entire house from the upstairs to the downstairs with it's distinctive tone. Both pouring in usual fear, they immediately put it aside and execute a quick plot knowing its probable that the phone call is incoming scheme in effect by their stalker.

- Listen you, answer the phone, while I'll check outside for him, this could be our one and only chance. Go !

ERNEST tells ALEX.

- Ok !

Pacing before the call drops, ALEX answers the phone.

- Who the fuck is this ?

Directly after his harsh phone presence is announced. Across the phone he reciprocates from the other side a womanly weep, first very soft but then gaining momentum. Trying to divulge who's doing the crying ALEX repeatedly asks "Hello" and "Who is this ?" Finally the moaning woman of mystery manages to mumble a few words out.

- Turn on the news, ALEX.

Gaining familiarity to the voice, ALEX calls out the suspecting woman by possible name, intending for a answer.

- CLARISSA !

He shouts. But she doesn't answer to the name, she ignores his confrontation and reiterates her last statement over. Sounding filled with emotion and held back pain.

- Just turn on the news, right now.

From the coffee table in the living room ALEX swipes the remote to press on and flickers through a few channels before landing on channel four late night news. Where broadcasting live at that hotel and where MOISSON SERVICES once stood as a profitable business and now as cradled brick, ashes, and soulless vessels littering everywhere like a holocaust. The reporter carries on in a passionate portrayal, delivering words to the death rattling damage almost near as the world we known had ended. It isn't within seconds where the channel airs to complete identical sketch drawings of himself and his father as prime suspects for not only that horrendous killing but for CUOCO'S and ANNABELLE'S too. The grand reward for any information and whereabouts about them uproots to fifty thousand. A pricey itch that some double crosser's would be too tempting to have surpass them.

Immediately ALEX goes into his explanation and deliberately promises that he's had nothing to do with anything that's being said he's committed against anyone. Pressing that it's all lies and that he's been framed. She doesn't want to hear it, and not in the case as she knows he's lying but under the standing that she isn't hinting towards that particular story.

- TURN TO NINE RIGHT NOW.

She delivers to him firm.

Pressing the forward button above the words "channel". He skims
through a few more stations and the television picture lands to it's
destination appointed. When it does, what he sees possesses him to
instantly to drop the remote from his hands on the stone hard floor where
the device's battery dissemble and discard there right at his feet on the
floor as everything transitions slow from his perspective. The voice over
the phone with as much volume they can conquer stricken with as much
ache and agony, fighting back tears that apparently must be fallen past
their cheeks, answers.

- DO YOU SEE...

The commotion from the fallen gadget captures ERNEST'S attention
from the outside and without a sight in anyone. He aids himself back in
where he sees ALEX there in the living room stuck in a standing
position as he moves closer to him. He watches as he begins to shield
his hand over his forehead like he's being hit with sun beams while
holding the phone in his other hand. ERNEST speaks out.

- What !... What's the matter, what's wrong now ?

Then he sees it, there in color casted all over the television like a portrait
in remembrance. It's a child and not only a child but ALEX'S son
BRADY picture there gleaming to life from the screen. Since the
afternoon while playing at the local park with friends, he disappeared
without anyone seeing or hearing anything from him accept that he was
last seen looking for his truck, a red fire truck that ALEX had just given
him for his fourth birthday. ERNEST looking on at the coverage running

his hands through his head, cloaked in the traumatic bombshell. Fueled with all these emotions and lost from words ALEX asks CLARISSA two questions before abandoning the phone to the floor quickly. "Are you home ?", "Stay there". Storming from the house after the phone call from CLARISSA and in goal to their home.

ALEX angrily raids speed in the passenger seat, while ERNEST with his hand to open the drivers tripping himself over something there in the driveway in adjacent to the car and with the sound of it scraping against the concrete it had to be some stick of metal of some sort. Doesn't matter with it being so dark outside you wouldn't be able to see it anyways. He gets inside and starts the car.

When pulling up outside from his home a detour he hadn't plan on was there to meet them in numbers. Two squad cars parked in front of the curb of his house twirling their red and blue lights that can be seen several blocks away is what's theorized. The first one sit vacant they must be in the company of CLARISSA already inside. The one behind is occupied and telling from the silhouette ALEX sees from his range there's two suspecting officers in the front seat.

ALEX extremely out of control with his nerves jacked up in suspiciousness asking his father in wonder with a ton of questions tossed at him. How much do they know already about him ? Are they there in hopes to capture him knowing he would come out of hiding for the return of his son ? Is CLARISSA informing him on his whereabouts ? Maybe it was wise he left his parents house when they did ?

ERNEST never answers his son's mirage of questions though even with them still coming at rapid rate. He just stares out from the windshield in angle to his house where the officers sit. Where the lights beam off his face in alarmed color patterns. ALEX in disarray going inside there now with highlight bulletins in warrants of arrest for him and his father would be suicide for his freedom. Not knowing what to do he contemplates exiting the car after ERNEST switches the headlights off after seeing the blue lights and pulls over to the curb a few blocks down from his house eyeing it from a distance. When ALEX notices his father seeming out of touch and incoherent to reality similar to him not caring, he pulls the handle from the door and attempts to step out. Once his foot touches outside the car, ERNEST with his right hand close, snatches a bulk of ALEX'S shirt in a knot and yanks him back into the car aggressively then shuts the door back close. ALEX looking on at his dad in disbelief that summons over his face in fear. Not understanding his actions so he asks in yells.

- DAD what the hell are you doing.

Out he cries.

- Look son I didn't want say this but this situation is out of ours hands, there is nothing we can do.

- What the hell your talking about dad, this is my son I'm talking about, your fucking grandson for god sakes. What you expect me to turn my back on him, is that it.

- Look I've held this in long enough and I never said a drop of it at strength of your mother.

-What the hell are you talking about ?

- We don't even know that's your son is what the hell I'm talking about. He don't look like you, me, or your mother maybe that skank fooled you into believing that was your son, just like she fooled you into marrying her once she got pregnant.

ALEX with instinct, extends his fist at his dad and connects to his nose with a power shot. ERNEST retaliates beastly by grabbing his son with both of his hands in miraculous strength and wrapping them around his throat with brutal force, strangling him as his nose drips with blood. ALEX struggling and fighting with all his might with ERNEST hands around his neck so viciously snug. You can hear this wrenching noise through his mouth in tune, the sound resonates with a rubber plunger unclogging a toilet. ERNEST hands are stomping down on his throat. ALEX eyes are filling with tears and finally gets a thought that can disrupt this maneuver that in any minute can take his life. He wills his leg in a swing to a upward motion between his father's leg catching his testicles with his knee fiercely. When the kick connects, out rings ERNEST'S shrieking high pitched roars that in accent it can favor a small boy who hurt himself falling down from his bicycle.

Not too far down the officers in the squad car sit quiet and reserved as back ups. The driver with his wandering eyes sets further down to the car where ERNEST and ALEX rumble in barbarically style and he can't help to see the foul play go on.

-I wonder what they do to your body when your slashed limb from limb like that CUOCO fucked from the commercials. What kind of funeral do you have ?

- You see that ?

- Where ?

- Right there in that car.

- What is that ? What's going on ?

- I don't know…but were going to find out.

Upon the release to the strangulation hold, ALEX gasps for more than one wind while serving his sore neck. ERNEST carries into his screams loud as he possibly can at the top of his lungs cupping both hands around his groin in pain and pure agony feeling the hurt settle in on his balls, fogging his entire driver's side window with his breath smoking whines. Which leads ALEX to him gripping his hand back on the door for his escape continuing his surge for more air as he slips down to the ground watching his father scream on and on in misery. Kicking the door to shut. In the middle of the street with his gun drawn in sights at ALEX, is the driver cop with his silent partner by his side as he shouts surrendering demands to him in the darkness calling for him to his feet with hands in the air slowly. Of course ALEX follows through in his harsh request, first getting to his feet but when he goes to put his hands up to the left is a clearing pass to a neighbor backyard he's frequent with. Without thinking and his neck throbbing in pain off he goes dashing in the darkness before lifting even one arm. The driver cop never shoots but gives pursuit in chase behind him on tail. ALEX hops pass a wooden fence beating the blue suit over in seconds as he's over and looks for what direction to sprint off from.

ERNEST in his excruciating pain remains intact to the situation. With the car engine still running and from the inside fogged with his breath from screaming. He shoots the gear in drive and jams his foot on the gas with hard pressure, zooming off with the tires screeching against the street and blasts through the passenger cop like a linebacker.

When the driver's side cop returns back to the street and scene, he watches almost as if its a pivotal part in a film to be seen. Witnessing his partner's full body (legs, arms, chest, and head) be trampled over monstrously killing him dead at the point of impact in a unbelievable sight. ERNEST unaware to his heinous actions after the collision and invests the thought to stop after but as he continues to coast down the street with his feet on the brake peddle isn't stopping, gunfire erupts and his rear window bursts in shatter from the outside, littering chunks of glass over the backseat. Looking past his shoulder out the broken rear shield with the car still moving, running as fast as he can with a service pistol in his hand is the drivers side cop giving chase to him in heavy sprint. Accountable to a end to his rear window in the process. ERNEST without capability to break, speeds up behind the wheel and makes it to the end of the street. As he pulls the stirring wheel to right as hard as he can for the turn to avoid clashing with civilian cars without the ability to slow down, he doesn't make it as planned and crashes the side of his car into some parked vehicles, luckily no one were in them. Eventually getting passed the vengeful cop and his fury of bullets. He jams his foot on the breaks several times as hard as he can, when looking down at his foot and he sees no results of the car slowing down. "WHAT THE FUCK" he shouts at the top of his lungs before placing his eyes back on the road in front of him. First he impales the car into a tree and knocks himself unconscious while his face explodes into his air bag. Fatally it looks.

In a far out spans that reaches forever the anthem of paramedics chime closer and closer. Freakishly not dead ERNEST basically in and out of the state of himself looks on as he's rescued from the torn wreckage that's left as his car. He's then placed on a gurney, bandage up from excessive bleeding from his head on down. Lifted off and strolled in goal to the rear of the ambulance as he sees a tandem of blue lights arriving all as a mob on the scene. Out from the head vehicle comes a distorted image striding directly towards him with a automatic in hand equipped to pull. Assuming it must be the cop who could had easily took half of his head off when firing those rounds that demolished his back window in pursuit to him on foot. Expectantly to get to his side with a gleaming low life smirk to assure his upcoming arrest even added to his self-caused impairment. Moments before that seem in a later occurrence. After he rammed into the tree. To his luck though , it isn't him raged in determination to his capture. As the individual moves in closer and ERNEST eyes stretch wider, the figure is the least expected person he intends on seeing in a moment like this. It's DAISY, at end of the gurney she touches his foot shedding tears down her face and rushes to him as ERNEST looks on and the feeling of exhilaration overwhelms his injured frame. DAISY holds him in her arms as he's lifted and propped inside the paramedic prepared to be taken off for further medical care. With DAISY caressing his head smiling down at him, the energy and vibe aids that everything is going to be fine in the instance even though everything is in the opposite. With the medics closing the door from the outside, shutting him off from the view of blue lights that go on forever in it's hovering. When it slams completely shut the noise of the closure doesn't match, instead of it being just one solid pound, for some reason a theme almost compared as an overbearing chain rattling surface in ERNEST hearing. He turns his head back up to DAISY and without saying anything. She look directly down at him and out comes two words but before she can finish the statement in her voice. Her words are saturated again with the loud jangling clatter of chains. Sounds of countless chains moving around, and around but what it entangles is unexplainable and unseen. ERNEST looks on in confusion at DAISY as her voice is weirdly substituted in exchange for the endless tone in serpent metals. He lip reads hers there with each other face to face and all he makes out is "I LOVE YOU" as his eyes drift folded from the faces and the lights, then into complete darkness. As the chain reaction in volume thrive on in a faded hearing until...

WOOOSH !

Rattled in a awakening in a solid chair from the flow of below
temperature water raining down in his face like a wave spiking you in
the deep ocean current. Blitzing away the blood that's stuck on his sores
from his cheek and forehead on accounts to the mega hit he took to the
tree after colliding with it.

Him coming to in the car, rescued by paramedics, with the blue suit
lights flickering around everywhere, and DAISY by his side was nothing
more than dream sleep during his unconsciousness. His reality is in a
much more demented in reverse.

ERNEST upon his rude conscious alerting, flustered strictly after
breathing heavily and deep almost as he drowned, finds himself confined
to a chair stripped to only his boxer drawers with his arms bound in
thick metal clamps bolted in a pad lock behind him in heavy duty
sheering silver torus shaped chains. Stretching in restraint from his
contracted wrist, then wrapped in bulges all around. From below his
waist to his neck. Displaying his upper portion to be a awful reminisce
in physical bondage as the Africans slaves had been captive and treated
on auction blocks sold for pennies in utter demoralization. Both even
sporting by the neck a genuine piece of vintage of american horror, a
iron slave collar with rods on the end pushing major inches and long
pointing spikes at its splitting ends. With ERNEST'S white skin
reflecting to the brightest in pink coloration, from the shackled chains
covering his body painting a mimicking resemblance to this country's
greatest shame even down to his ankles being clamped down on steel
cold metal clamps attached to the end legs of the chair.

Bewildered, dazed, and disoriented to his current scene, his face pouring from water and fear. Shackled like a dog to a chair in a pitch dark room where the only visible surroundings is under a bright dangling light aiding only his existence with its tingling bright flash. So disoriented ERNEST doesn't even realizes his son ALEX beside him calling out to him "Dad" who's also too confined in the same measures of extremity bound from head to toe in metal connected loops spiraled around him in his near nakedness excluding underwear. Propped in the chair emerging himself to be in the most uncomfortable positioning as the weight of the chains bearing down his entire upper body causing him to slant his self in awkward left and right positions. ERNEST in desperate intel to where they are ? How they've gotten there ? And who put them there ? Comes in urgent to his tone and delivery where you can blatantly articulate the colossal level of dread he had when he spoke his words.

- Where the hell are we ? I can feel my breath struggling to my lungs to breathe.

ERNEST states.

Doing his best to try and consider how much can he motion in his confined seating. Wiggling, squeezing, shaking, and jerking are all helpless to his current disposition, the more he moves the more it seems the chains become tightened. Lending more ache and displeasure. Meanwhile ALEX exposes the last thing he remembers before waking and finding himself there next to his father, barreled in endless metal straps.

He begins back on the street after their fight inside the car and the cop ordering him to place his hands in the air. But he shoots off and beats the cop that's behind him over the gate and then rushes as fast as he can without looking back down a dark alley where he stops at a merge to a sidewalk. When he does, like a rumble he hears gunshots rang out that sounds as if they had to have came from the previous space he was in. But as he's turning around in that direction. To the back of his head he feels a shot and like a light switch, he goes out.

- Next thing I know I wake up to a bucket of freezing water in my face with my head spinning around like I took enough pills to end it all. And you beside me. I feel drugged, whoever put us here drugged us dad, you feel drugged ?

ALEX asks.

- Your not drugged, that's head trauma.

- What ?

ALEX asks.

- You ain't under the influence, its a concussion. You said in the alley you heard shots.

- Right !

- Before you could turn around, you went out.

- Yea !

- Someone blindsided you and knocked you out. Turn your head a little so I can see.

ALEX does as his father insists on. Not even in a full angle as he shifts his head there's a trail of blood raining down the back of his neck and even down to the chains like a stream. Shifting fully around, the damage is much worst viewing practically his son's head flesh caved in, having to be from the workings of some heavy solid instrument by whoever responsible for their placement there. ERNEST reaction to the blow speaks for itself.

- OOOOH MY GOD ALEX.

ERNEST reacts bending his down ashamed.

- What ? What's wrong.

- Somebody opened you up good. And they probably struck a nerve when doing it, without no doctor your bound to bleed to death. Quick ! Tell me do you feel anything, anything at all.

ERNEST words in deep concern.

- I don't feel anything. What it looks like he hit me with...

- It doesn't fucking matter all that does is you need help...

Out from the encircling darkness a sound from a door shuts then comes a calm but assertive male voice that commands ALEX and ERNEST'S attention away from themselves and into the dimness in hopes to place a voice with a face. Snapping his broad feet against the hard bald floor in pace towards the two hindered ones from the shadows...

- Twenty eight inch, twenty ounce copperhead, aluminum strength bat. The best your is money worth.

...he's revealed. Medium in height, slim but a sturdy mold, youthful in the face, and stunting a dark complexion that breaks even with his black long sheering trench jacket that rolls down to his calf distinctive to a cape. Cuffing his hands in his coat as he steps fully into the light so that they can see him from top to bottom. With each of their eyes sinking in on one another. The standing figure showcasing intimidation, as ALEX and ERNEST reflect plea in a mixture of adversity.

ERNEST quickly spills out his perception wasting no time.

- Your DOUBLE R aren't you.

He says as if they can be his last words from his mouth.

- MOSS told you who he was...he laying back under that bed in the apartment. You don't remember ERNEST.

Disarranging airs ERNEST face entirely, lost for words at the standing figure's knowledge that it even takes him a secondary moment to conjure memory of.

- If your not DOUBLE R motherfucker who are you and why do you have us chained here. Why did you killed ANNABELLE, and CUOCO, and MOSS massacring those others in that bomb trick you son of bitch.

Interrupting his sons gathered questions and interjecting his own before the standing figure could give his explanation is ERNEST.

- And why the hell are you hunting us down, trailing us like the fucking reaper, notes here, notes there. What the hell we do to you. I don't know you, I haven't harmed you.

ERNEST says with ALEX overwhelmed with emotion so much his face streams down in tears, doing his best to muscling around restrained.

- You sure about that ?

The standing figure responds back calmly with his eyes piercing directly on the two of them. ALEX pays ample attention held down bolted with chains around him watching as his eyes click left and right sensing there has to be something more with this character. As he looks on at his father, struggling to grip a breath from the tie down on his body due to the chains. Tears shoots down from the corners of his eyes, and aloud like a child he screams in poor cries.

- WHO THE FUCK ARE YOU ? PLEASE TELL ME WHO THE FUCK ARE YOU ?

His infant behavior that doesn't seem to be staged or incorporated as a pity move. It has no affect or remorse in the standing figure's empathy as he just fixes his focus on them still obviously with his mind made up to his judgement. No different to a officer interrogating a suspect. Resisting any statement or action that comes from his pre-guilt mouth.

- Soooo...the big mystery is who am I ? Lets just say for the moment I'm a person who's killed a helluva a lot people to stand in the same room as you two motherfuckas.

Choosing his statement that approaches ERNEST in exact.

- Me...excuse me sir, and I mean that at the most sincerity. I think you got it all wrong. Maybe you have me mistaken...me and my son mixed with some other person who's bestowed a grudge you decided to take in claim and I don't blame you. But whatever they did, had no involvement with us sir. We're good people, I-I have house in Tenleytown with my wife, I'm clicking retirement in two years, I love Magic Johnson. Can we please just talk about this, whatever this is we can talk about this.

ERNEST persists himself in.

ALEX next to him begins to experience some different functions, as his body begins to slow down and his face shades more bright to pale almost once he comes down from whimpering. Drifting his head in a downward spiral as it almost begins to hang like a slinky. His continuance to lose blood on his body is beginning to take affect finally.

ERNEST doing his best to offer anything hanging from a short piece of string that's his life. Believes he had gotten over to the STANDING FIGURE as he moves in close toward him, hoping he can possibly release them from their bondage. The man positions himself in front of ERNEST'S legs standing in front of him crowding his shadow like a larger than life force. ERNEST pleads with him again and the man removes his hands from his pockets and proceed in a few combinations with his fist then commences to wailing them to ERNEST'S face. Tapping his mouth to the point that once he's finished waving his hand away from the blows. ERNEST spits away blood boiling in saliva from his mouth on to the bare floor from the rapid punches. A cut on his cheek sheds drops of his blood down his face.

There's a bucket of water the standing figure snatches and dumps in ERNEST'S face in hopes to relieve him from being unconsciousness after the hard blows to his face but all it does is sheer the blood away momentarily. He does the same to ALEX who's nearly out of it himself the way his head dangles.

Remaining in front of him as ERNEST waves his head around euphorically, dizzy from the punches. The standing figure then from his pockets reveals several papers and collects a few of them before placing the others back into his pocket collectively. On one of the papers as he shuffle through, he goes and stands himself over ALEX who recollects from the bucket shower to his face and he recites out information loud and clearly.

- ALEXANDER BENJAMIN ST.CLAIR
3742 YUMA STREET. State yes or no for confirmation.

Still out of trance and appearing sickly. Pained with his face turning blue-ish from the heavy slips of blood loss growing rapidly. ALEX doesn't respond to the standing figures commanding statements, which leads to him reciting them over.

ERNEST looking on barely conscious himself, turns his neck that's growing stiff from the weight of the chains over to his son and sees the turmoil speaking in so many words to his fading complexion. He pleads to the man to show mercy on his son in his state near death.

- Leave the kid alone, you nearly took a chunk from the back of his head out when you hit him. Look at him he's losing blood by pints for christ sakes.

There isn't any sympathy for ALEX and his vital injuries in the heart of the controlling hand. The STANDING FIGURE tries his best in getting ALEX to comprehend and respond to his demands. Particularly by smacking him in the face constantly which isn't successful but does anger ERNEST so much he shouts for him to stop then calls upon himself to call out to his son for revival.

- ALEX... ALEX... ALEX, wake up.

The STANDING FIGURE sees that even his technique isn't registering to ALEX so he invests in a idea where he goes off into the darkness and returns back with a bottle in his hand. ERNEST curious and worried to what it is he has in the clear container that poses him to step in the back of ALEX'S head where his bad wound lies, gushing in flesh. Troubled to what it looks as if he's about to do next. He calls out.

- What the hell are you doing ? Stop it... leave him alone.

The STANDING FIGURE loosens the top of the container on the bottle with the label in little bold words entitling it as "RUBBING ALCOHOL". He then pours the liquid inside onto ALEX'S wound. The instant pain triggers his reaction to scream out at the top of his lungs like he's been resuscitated back to life, screaming out in pain as his clear and hard tone in moans must dwell beyond the dungeon surroundings they linger to in the moment.. Tears shoot down from ERNEST'S eyes as he looks on cringing, shuffling around in the chains barely with enough strength to even move a length. He douses more of the alcohol onto his gash, watching as the blood and antiseptic mixture creep in flow down ALEX'S scalp with him prolonging in his outcry enduring the painful misery subjected by torture.

Following the anti biotic head bath in sadistic measures that redeems ALEX'S blood loss and cures him from his suffering dizziness. The STANDING FIGURE wastes no time in forcing ALEX face to face with the alcohol still in hand as a harsh reminder to identify with his question that he previously insisted him to answer. And after his last volatile experience fixed in bitter ache he has no choice or problem this final time, so he does what he's told and he confirms the question to be valid in his repeating. Accomplishing his agenda set upon ALEX first, he switches his eyes to ERNEST as second. He props himself in front of him and no different than the same inquest he displayed against ALEX. He pushes it now onto ERNEST as he daringly looks at him in the face with everything in hateful vengeance, in his stare he curses the figure in anyway imaginable, knowing he is completely helpless to his bidding. But was not going to surrender when questioned.

The figure brandishes more of the papers from his coat pocket and posts them up in billboard style to ERNEST'S face.

- Who and what name ? What address am I holding in this picture ?

The STANDING FIGURE voices as he remains determined in his full badger mode blazing his eyes down on ERNEST, who's vulnerable to his questioning expectations, as he returns the favor. And in return ERNEST does seated there with nothing he can do or anywhere to go with this piece of paper at the tip of his nose holding a distinct copy of his drivers license identification card detailing all his personal information. Typical information, the natural thing to do would be for him to verify the sheet as him. But he doesn't, he knows he and his son are hanging on their last string before death at this deranged unknown hands, his thoughts circling is above being tortured like dogs. He rather die, he takes one last look at the paper then at the figure with eyes dead set on him to concur to his question that he goes into repeating once more. ERNEST instinctually with much spite spits at the picture and calls for the killer to shoot him in a attempt to reclaim honor before he dies.

Calling to his bluff, miraculously he gets his wishes also as the STANDING FIGURE pauses in the moment then removes his self backwards a few steps. From his pocket he draws out his piece; a thirty-eight revolver unhesitant in doing as if its a stick of gum, and then fires it in a low angle at ERNEST. POOOWWW! Striking a shot straight in his knee cap with the bullet lodging in. Then watches good in deserving as ERNEST barks and moans relentlessly struggling and shuffling with the chains rattling in suffocation around him. As blood running all down his leg forming a thick nauseating red puddle at the ball of his foot. ALEX looks on with tears of mercy in his eyes in plea to be let go as his father huffs and puffs in manly screams from a hole bigger than a cough drop grossly covers his left knee in aftermath damage. Even more determined now that ERNEST realizes how far he's willing to go by putting a round in him. The STANDING FIGURE scrambles for the paper with ERNEST'S personals down on the floor painted in tiny streaks of blood. He secures it and jams it in ERNEST'S face smothering him with it as he mumbles over the paper wrinkles and red splatters with one hand. While his other aims his heat at his foot and promises another bullet round there and assures him he'll make sure he gags his son as he sits and watches as he bleeds out to death in front of him. Only if he plans on resisting one more time as he sets firm on his point making.

He offers one final opportunity slinging back the trigger for ERNEST to agree that the paper does indeed hold his information in front of his eyes. Deceasing the consistent phrases that their current plight in torture are mix ups and mistakes on the case of not only his identity but his sons very well also. Putting to rest ERNEST'S countless notions that supposedly the standing figure has made an huge error in his abduction. With his mind made up the crucial character counts down from five before invoking his promise to inflicting serious harm against ERNEST that will lead to his demise.

- FIVE... FOUR... THREE...

Just before he hits the number two, you hear out at the top of his lungs in cries with his mouth buried in crinkled paper. ERNEST at last gives into the STANDING FIGURE'S bitter request. Shouting in claims that the identity presented is in fact himself in fear of his life taken. Giving into one helluva compromise, the paper is removed from his face for full comprehension to his speech.

- ALRIGHT... ALRIGHT it is me. Please just don't kill me or my son. ITS ME GOTDAMMIT... IS THAT WHAT YOU WANNA HERE.

- I want to hear you state it, tell me who you are, and your address as loud as possible. Say it right now muthafucka.

Coughing and steady trying to breathe in and out, clinched tighter than a knot from the chains. Reciting ERNEST does while staring at the barrel of the STANDING FIGURE'S gun remaining to point downward in direction at his right foot as he stare down at him in his eyes watching his compliance to every word.

- I'M ERNEST BENJAMIN ST. CLAIR, 3234 UTAH AVENUE.

- GOOD...now there shouldn't be any more discussion or questioning my judgement as to why your here MR. ST.CLAIR. And now with that out of the way, it's time for me to tell you why I brought you here and got them chains around you.

Collecting the paper copy with ERNEST'S identification intel, scraggly from the wear, used in advantage practices. He folds it back up and places back into his pocket. While savaging that piece out he comes with another paper folded neatly into the shape of a triangle, in the color gray. It's a newspaper and judging by the both of them looking on, the paper has a bit of age on it with the way he handles it delicately. Folding it out it lengths a minor article in his hand as he stares as goes into reading under the headlining picture bold in portrait above the lettering.

" A drowning day in tears covers the emotions of a never ending crowd, gathered altogether holding a candle behind a alley where all but a day ago. This is where a older gentlemen subjected to homelessness discovered in the nearby dumpster where the group rally in prayers. A body wrapped in cloth dead and abandoned. That body belong to all city player Robert Rocket, who was listed as one of the main three top players in high school looking to be recruited for the country's elite school's collegiate basketball teams. Rocket grew to local fame after reaching three triple fifty point plus games a month before, and it was rumored he was asked to work out with a few of the players of the native BULLETS team in the future. But unfortunately his family would have to make arrangements to service his funeral for his unexpected departure than draft day attire. Reports state oddly in his autopsy that the young ball sensation was stripped from his clothes top to bottom. Reports also in detail spoke on how his body was severely bruised with strange markings on his flesh that resemble chains. Even more gruesome there's statement saying he was opened surgically, split wide from his chest and waist. Where multiple essential organs were said to be discovered missing. " FEBRUARY 10, 1980

Immediately after the briefing of the story ALEX catches on to the insinuation by the STANDING FIGURE that perhaps they're culpable to the victim in the story. His reading for sharing.

- ROBERT ROCKET who is that ? You think we had something to do with what happened to that kid in the article ? I don't know what your talking about and this is my first time even hearing about that story. Right Dad !

ALEX says with enthusiasm (appearing honest).

Wondering his eyes elsewhere except towards this intimidating character and for the first settling amongst the weight of the chains ERNEST without reinforcement he does posing in a mood of guilt. As the STANDING FIGURE watches his bodily movement that indicates his awareness fully to the story.

- Right Dad ! …you don't know anything about a ROBERT ROCKET do you ? Not even him being a possible first round draft pick ? Or coming out of High school to play professional, now he's just another corpse in the ground because his life along with the organs in his body was taken from him at only seventeen years old. No, no, no ALEX …I think your dad knows exactly what the fuck I'm talking about to this story. DON'T YOU ERNEST TELL THE TRUTH !

The STANDING FIGURE words in a tempo from calm to angrily.

ALEX looks over at his father who's budging around in his seat as the chains rattle over and over like a lullaby. Indecisive from it being his fear to his knowledge of the story or the gunshot wound to his knee that's still pouring from his leg. In silence awaiting for ERNEST to verify a answer to the question, the STANDING FIGURE and ALEX both look on in momentum for different opinions.

ALEX in expectancy that his father doesn't concur to his awareness of any of the story because in his perspective they're innocent from all the deranged accusations pinned against them by the abductor. While the STANDING FIGURE burns his eyes directly at ERNEST with his aura vengeful in his pursuit for the truth.

Finally after his son skeptically asking. ERNEST feels driven to answer from the pressure holding back all he can looking over to ALEX first then the STANDING FIGURE'S face and in reply to the question he says.

- No !

- There's your answer now can you please, please let us go.

The STANDING FIGURE looks on after ERNEST'S reaction and in his face he has disappointment in expectancy of some sort all over his face. As ERNEST stares back, it takes a second but he fades into the pitch black background gone to the unknown stepping off.

In his brief absence ALEX opens himself into questioning his father prolonged answer. Unworried but curious to the blatant hesitation.

- Dad is there anything you want to tell me ?

- I love you son, no matter what I love you.
In a long pause after.

- You sure nothing else.

ALEX asks.

- What ?

- He motioned to you.

- So what does that mean ?

- It means I have eyes and I'm not blind to his questions dad the way he was signaling it was to you, directly to you almost. Almost as if he's know you or you know him.

- What are you asking me ALEX ? Now is not the time or fucking place to do this. We need to be trying to invest our heads together and figure out a way to getting out of here.

- What about you ?

- What about me ALEX, what the fuck are you talking about now.

- Back when I first told you about ANNABELLE you asked me did I have anybody, anybody at all as enemies who would do something like this to spite me for my past...PAST DEMONS TO BE EXACT. I want to know do you ?

ALEX utters staring directly at his father in desperate seriousness for him to answer.

- We don't have time for this shit, not right now.

Wiggling and struggling bound by the chains he replies.

- No dad, its not our time anymore its his...

Referencing to the STANDING FIGURE they're held captive too cemented in his forsaken pit. Jamming his neck and head in the last direction he stood.

On the verge of finalizing his statement, out from the shadows very much like a dream arises ALEX'S young son BRADY. Standing there in place with the accessible wall of dark behind him, beholding to the light raining down on him. Looking over at his father fidgeting around with what seems to be a toy in his hand. ALEX and ERNEST doubtful looking back at the boy, their inner feelings touch them both the same and alike from their facial responses that this moment can't be authentic.

Immediately pausing comes to play, and before the silence carries on and tells his son depart. ALEX calls out to him and he answers.

- Hey daddy, Hey granddad!

- Hey son.

- I got a toy...you see it.

- It's a real nice toy son. Daddy wants you to tell him where is the man who brought you here.

- He's outside.

Pointing his finger backwards towards the darkness.

- So there's a door ?

ERNEST says.

- Where's the door ?

His son points back in the direction once again.

- Listen buddy, I'm a need a big favor, and you've done favors for me before right.

ALEX says.

- RIGHT !

- Daddy is gone to need you to try and help him get his hands out these handcuffs, so he can free granddad and then we all can leave for ice cream. Now how's that sound buddy, can you do that for me.

His son nods his head yes in agreement to his ALEX'S much needed favor.

- Put the toy down son, and come help your dad.

His son follows his commands. He places the toy down slowly on the ground in front of him and before he can take a few steps in mission. A arm creeping grips over his shoulder pulls him back softly and in from the dimness revealing a face feast with fierce is the STANDING FIGURE. Holding his arm around ALEX'S son shoulder like a friendly companion, stagnating his intentions to ordering his son in his only chances of freedom.

- You won't leave a friend, would you ?

The STANDING FIGURE complies to his son. Who shakes his head side to side phrasing the gesture "no".

- Daddy this is my friend. He gave me my new toy see.

ALEX nearly looses himself as he watches on as his young innocent son stand side by side with a man more than a menace. His thoughts race him to the worst outcome imaginable the STANDING FIGURE may have in mind. Furious to his contact, ALEX goes straight forward in his threatening being as cold and earnest as can be with his eyes straightforward, face tightening from animosity, and his head to the neck up stiff from bearing the chain weight.

- YOU HEAR ME LOUD AND CLEAR YOU BLACK
MOTHERFUCKER. IF YOU AS SO MUCH HARM A HAIR ON MY
SON'S HEAD. GIVING CHANCE WHEN I GET FROM THIS CHAIR
YOUR GOING TO WISH YOU PUT A BULLET IN ME MORE
SOONER, AND I FUCKIN PROMISE THAT.

- You promise that, huh ?

- TRY ME !

ALEX responds.

Reserved and quiet in response, the STANDING FIGURE drops his
head down at BRADY. Who stands there remaining in tuned to his toy
in hand, disclosed from his father's vulgarity in verbal protection.

With his left arm in place over the small young's shoulder. ALEX and
ERNEST stare off in opposite view at this lunatic's next movement that
by his demeanor he's leaning next in the direction of doing something
berserk to the child, that cringes the two of them even before it happens.
With his lefty over the boy from the far it scrambles out of place at first
without his right in his frame. But when out from the darkness like a
trick he pours his other arm, his right hand on the kids shoulder. Only
this one is flashing that nickel plated beauty, with the chrome
shimmering slowly as he places it there provoking his potential ability as
an indirect message through action at ALEX in vision to his prior
threats.

ALEX with no possible in rescuing BRADY from the position he's too
young and immature to understand. So he begins to begging with his
terrifying shadow hovering over his son to not do anything to hurt his
son, as tears shoot down from his eyes and saliva burst from mouth,

ERNEST assists in the pleading.

- PLEASE I'M BEGGING YOU ... I'M PLEADING YOU WITH NOTHING TO BARTER BUT MY LIFE IN EXCHANGE FOR THAT BOY'S. DON'T DO IT.

ALEX tells.

- He's only a child, please don't do this. I know what you are, we know who you are. PLEASE ! YOU DONT HAVE TO DO THIS.

ERNEST also states.

The STANDING FIGURE with his right hand palmed around his strap, finger not yet so prone to scratch his itch at his index as the barrel nearly touches his neck. BRADY adjusting from his attention to his child entertainment and now peeping his eyes directing to his father and grandfather's forced placement.

Taking in their words to deter his suspected motives. He responds in return opposite to a probable thought that they may have.

- You got me all wrong. I don't hurt everybody or anyone especially a child. If you thinking I would do what you thought, your wrong...

Under his voice ERNEST whispers the word "nigger" in response to the abductor negating the relations to him a heartless killer.

- ...just because your killer doesn't mean you don't have a conscience fool.

He then escorts ALEX'S son to a chair amongst the bright circle under the dangling light. In the close proximity to ERNEST.

Then after he moves himself perfectly back to the place from which he stood before, he begins to reword himself again sort of to his last statement.

- I don't believe in hurting a child or a elder. You know why ? Because it is said they're the closest lives we have on earth to the creator...but I can't say I won't spare this though.

He steps off back into the darkness for a few seconds and flashes before the both of them like a prize. Shoving BETSY, ERNEST'S wife and ALEX'S mother to the floor under the light. She's handcuffed and gagged at the mouth where she can mutter words distortedly. The STANDING FIGURE picks her up from the floor as she screams incoherently, and jams his gun to her temple with her eyes running a puddle of tears in extreme fear hearing him lunge back the trigger " CLICK" next to her skull as the excitement roar.

- All jokes aside now ERNEST, they all took they ass home. I want the truth right here and right now. And I ain't got no problem blowing this bitch head off right in front of you or that little boy over there. So what you wanna do ? Because if you gon keep blowing smoke, I might as well right along with you.

ERNEST screams "BETSY", while ALEX shouts "MOM".

With ALEX'S little son looking on sharing head turns in each direction, panicking to the sight. Seeing a gun pointed to his grandmother's head, but unknown and incapable to do anything the young boy just sits there parked in his seat watching the chaos go on before him. As the weight of the moment has him under clear chilled shock.

The gun hasn't fired a single round, although it did appear the outcome would quickly escalate to that decision. Instead the STANDING FIGURE gropes DAISY at the back of her neck so roughly her eyes shoots to the back. As he forces her nearer to the knees of her husband and son as they sit constrained.

DAISY fallen to floor manages to turn over and with her eyes screeching out in need for help. She looks over at ALEX who helplessly can do nothing in aid to his mother, but pour tears from his eyes while cursing him worst to his ability allows. For sometime growing tired and sick of ALEX'S mouth, the abductor steps toward to him as he's ranting and swings the barrel at his mouth twice and busts his mouth open, blood rushing down in full flow from his wounded lips. The others look on in fright to the brutality, DAISY closes her eyes haven't can't bear to take a look at the viewing of her son being trounced on savagely.

She steers her eyes when the STANDING FIGURE finishes with ALEX over to ERNEST and communicative in her sight to him, he reads her cry out for help from him with her face drenched in sweat, clothes rugged with dirt, and her eyes covered in what looks to be a forever ending grief. To save their family from dreaded execution which soon will arrive on the time bought by the kidnapper. There before her face he regrets putting her life on the line like this. His pain leads him to droplets of tears down his cheeks.

The STANDING FIGURE then orders DAISY to her feet which becomes a challenge within itself being that her hands are handcuffed backwards, making the command almost impossible for her to act on. He realizes and then aids her to her feet.

ALEX delirious enough to barely summon his vision like before swings his head back and forth in a motion pained pretty bad from the facial beating he's just got. Wasting no time showing his level that discards any feeling to any of his torture upon them. The abductor now with DAISY standing, puts her at the head of ERNEST'S feet with his eyes all on her as he presses his gun again right at her head, right in front of his face. Dismantling his manhood as a husband blatantly in front of his helpless wife.

In realization to his weak disposition ERNEST begins to turn away his eyes from his wife held captive under this madman's hands. DAISY muttering, screeching, and humming with his gun to her head boils too much for him to see. With it all glaring down in his face, the STANDING FIGURE sees his coward negations and calls him out.

- DON'T TURN AWAY FROM ME, Don't turn away from your wife. Look at her... LOOK AT HER I SAID.

He shouts deepening his voice in anger. That snaps ERNEST attention to his command. When he turns looking at his wife there, knowing at any moment by the pull of that trigger, she can be gone, it does something to his eyes. You can see his ego conquered but the taunting from the abductor doesn't end.

- Your going to tell me what I know you know. Only I want it said in front of everybody in this room, do you understand me ?

- Know what ?...I don't have even slightest fucking idea, what your talking about. I've told and told you have it all wrong.

ERNEST replies

Impatient to his ordained lies erupts the STANDING FIGURE powerfully when he tosses DAISY aside leaving her to drop hard to the floor when he kicks ERNEST in his bloody gunshot wounded knee that sends him screaming out in unimaginable agony. Echoing the room with his roars, the torture isn't yet finished when ERNEST catches a heavy punch to his face, switching hands from his piece he does.

Evolving more vicious in his position, ridding himself of the calm he once had before. DAISY lying on the ground again looks over at ALEX with his head sticking over to his shoulder almost as he's unconscious, but gains some will to peep back at his mom, when she's yanked back to her feet from the ground by the abductor and his barrel smiling at her between the eye and nose.

ALEX in a stage that makes him appear unaware to his deadly surroundings but behind him with his hands contained and restricted in metal cuffs, without the abductor suspecting he's on the verge of slipping his thin wrists free. A large step that revitalize the idea of him very possibly becoming a factor in garnering a escape as soon as possible.

Dazed and breathing in and out rapidly from the pain shooting through his knee from the kick. The STANDING FIGURE pressures ERNEST again, doing the most damage he plans ahead of time to make ERNEST comply to his wanted questions.

- TELL ME WHAT I WANT TO KNOW RIGHT NOW...

He demands in the straightest face to ERNEST with his gun in hand without any tremble against the back of DAISY'S head. She's mumbling annoyingly behind the cloth stuffed in her mouth blinking her tears opening and closing her eyes awaiting the blast and the bullet penetrating experience to send her off. ERNEST clutched from the kick and his eyes locked in on his wife. His hawking her throws him off to the question he was asked by the abductor and when he takes too long his consequences result with a bash to his face with a gun in a reflex motion. The blow knocks his head awkwardly in angle that leaves him in disorder.

- SAY IT ?

The STANDING FIGURE cries out.

Young BRADY over in the chair stands by observing everything in a stance of unknown and concern. His premature inability to process what he's witnessing resonates to wrong doing but his fear isolates him to the seat pressuring him to continue to look on.

ERNEST still restrained blood covering his face with multiple fleshy scars carved into his face even still from the car wreck. Grown tired of the constant strike and torture at the hands of the STANDING FIGURE. Something inside of him as he picks his head up in dizziness calls out before he's thought to be hit again.

-Alright, alright, alright. Please I'll tell you what I know, all I ask is one thing, one fucking thing... LEAVE MY FAMILY ALONE ?... and, How did you find me ?

DAISY hears his words looking on at him and her trembling lessens as she feels he drops his piece from her head. Even ALEX turns his eyes lazy over at his father overhearing, while struggling and scraping his wrist to the bone to unbound his hands locked behind him.

A small amount in alleviation spreads over the abductor's face. Could it be from ERNEST'S face to admittance after the chronic tension in questioning that collided with merciless repercussion he's undergone from this maniacal assassin.

The abductor letting go of DAISY from his hands and as she falls to the hard cold floor in a grunt. He stares dead at ERNEST with his feet planted to the floor frozen in movement. As one last time he repeats his last recounted question chiming over from his exhausted breath. And the abductor hanging on to letting it flow past him melodically, the question shifting him into a memory capsule of his. A place that examines an answer.

7.CHAPTER

FLASHBACK--

Seated there the STANDING FIGURE is on a bus trailing it's daily route through the misty rainy streets. Eyes sunken from pain, and his face curdling with hurt. Ahead of the bus he recognizes a woman chewing down a red apple, crunching every piece with him watching carefully reminding him as her mouth moves up and down in eating gracefully in slow motion. Outside he turns his head to his window and as the bus moves from a stop request he catches a glimpse of few kids running presumably to escape the showers of rain hailing down. As fast as they can with one of the kids, a boy that's ahead with the group dribbles a basketball hurrying down the block lugging his gym bag looking as if the storm doesn't even bother him. Gazing on these two more than life scenarios playing out begin to affect him deeply grabbing hold of his feelings. He begins to choke up even more when he turns in a opposite direction to his window peeping pass just before he misses a look at some school as its pictured to him with his eyes beaming at it like a skyscraper in seconds and just another landmark behind the next. When it's gone a emptiness strikes him and down his head goes sunken into his hands. A obituary program from the funeral of a ROBERT ROCKET, there in front is his picture holding his gym bag and jersey number commemorating his beloved image to all.

A pamphlet size folding handed out to all attendees at his last farewell go off. Freshly sitting there as miles and miles of processing and images run through his mind particularly in his previous sightings. Holding too much in the moment. When from nowhere out comes a voice at him, soft but very close from a female.

- Excuse me...hello are you gonna be ok ?

She kindly asks.

He lifts his head to the lovely voice matching a young woman seated in front of him, turning herself backwards seated but can't help to sense that he must've had some problems by energy vibes and curious to she might could help somehow. Viewing by the moisture red in his eyes her prognosis was correct.

- Excuse me, I don't mean to be in your business but I'm sitting right here in this seat in front of you and something told me to turn around and now that I did I can see why.

The girl was brightest in black from her complexion. And her hair was real short and well styled, different in looks but attractive in appeal.

- No it's cool I'm just sitting here with a lot on my mind. And this rain got me more in my feelings than I'm already am.

He tells her.

- I can tell you lost someone ?

- Yea he could of been ?

- What ?

- Nothing, never mind.

He says to her. Sinking his head back down at the pictures covering the program.

The girl beginning to latch on his distancing, hops from her seat and slides next to him racing to see what he has in his lap that's holding him more attention than her.

- Can I see ?

Peeping into his space with him showing a feel of privacy, but gives a opening to her. There lying flat between his legs in his hands is at the obituary, she grabs with his consent peeping directly at the photo in familiarity slightly in one point but then handing it back right away. Almost as she wished she never even bothered to look.

- I can't imagine what it's like to lose someone...

She says consoling.

- You can't see...

He tells her directly.

- See what ?

She asks.

- I guess you haven't heard...do you know who's in picture.

-No, tell me who is it ?

-This is ROBERT ROCKET, he was one of the top five recruit ball players in the entire country. Estimations from all over even greats saying he was going to be the next best basketball player that the NBA's ever seen...he was.

Pointing at the picture telling her.

Seeing how down he is and the photo of ROCKET gazing back at her there in his hands. A feeling in removal overcomes her, thinking to maybe just play as if this is the next stop and desert the confrontation altogether. Just before she slips her hand on the cord over the crushed young man as he keeps his head down and eyes fixed on the photo of ROCKET blanketed in his pain. He turns over to her, face to face, eye to eye, heart both beating as one. Right as she lifts to stand, he grabs her hand.

- My bad...I know something in you telling you right now to get the fuck away from this nigga but everything in me just sore right now. And I don't no what way or other way to process this shit.

Resisting all the strength kindling towards him and his strong emotions. She finally gives in to him and cradles his hands with empathizing in most sincerity in her compassion while clinging his hands in time of dreadful need.

Introductions swap come naturally after, she tells him her name is DIANE and he tells her his name is DWAYNE. In short time everyday they grow closer with each other talking out and about like friends laughing and joking. Suddenly the pain from the loss of ROCKET isn't all that bad anymore, the ways of life takes its course and DWAYNE even begins to forget about it, accepting the realities of how things are when your living and then you've spent the ordained time you were supposed to have spent here on earth. The natural orders with a male and female grip the two and before they know it, the special moment in sharing they're first kiss comes upon in only a month. Then looking on everything just seems the way it should be, two young people who just so happened to have found themselves into each other lives to embark in sharing happiness and care with one another. That is until...

Lying around in DIANE'S apartment one regular afternoon in front of the television beside her. Out the from hall at the door comes a knock, its expected when DIANE races to answer. A little more than a half a hour before, the two got hungry and decided to ordered a pizza. Still on the bed hypnotized by the television is DWAYNE while DIANE unlatches the lock on the door for the delivery guy for a brief greeting and then deepening her hands into her pockets for the fare. Being that she doesn't has it and probably has forgotten it, she yells out back at the room to a snugged up DWAYNE pressing the remote.

- Hey baby !

- Yea...

- Look in the closet please and bring my purse.

- Aite !

Hopping up from bed the second after asking. DWAYNE proceeds to her closet and spreads his eyes for her purse, that isn't a easy find stumbling into the space cluttered in female clothes. But is eventually found lying down on top of what looks to be some old worn out bag that isn't suited with the other belongings. DWAYNE stoops down and swipes the bag in his hand like no big deal. But when he lifts it from off top of the other bag below it, he recognizes the bag on her closet floor not just being any average bag. It's a gym bag and more important than the distinction to the item's name. The gym bag triggers familiarity as he stares down at the logo, when he eases back into the closet on his knees to the floor seeking a closer view, touching it, and moving it around slightly with his fingers. He realizes it isn't just any gym bag, rummaging around he unzips it open gently with goosebumps.

Meanwhile DIANE there at the door stands awkwardly in front of the delivery guy who is just as impatient as her while she waits for DWAYNE to finally bring her the bag like she asked, with more moments dragging and breeding frustration she calls out to him again only this time louder as a reminder.

DWAYNE hears but disregards her calls as he's consumed to the contents inside this mysterious frequent gym bag that connects with him closely almost as if it has been his at one time. But these items are a little different than most things in a regular old gym bag that someone uses for sports or activities. Everything it contains isn't typical or the average possessions that would exist inside any locker gym bag. He does find a shirt, a pair shorts, and towel. But digging more deeper through he also discovers more things that are obviously unrelated having to be inside of a gym bag. Things like a few pens, a old red rotten apple, a history book that looks to belong to a school. DWAYNE searches it's history associate index inside and along with two prior names the book has been issued too. The current name is initialed " R.R " the date reaching back nearly a year ago. Eerily to him he reserves himself after the disclosure.

Still at the door the delivery guy has past reached his level in patience. So before marching off with the impression of DIANE not paying for the pizza. He tells her.

- Look I only got a hour left on my shift before I'm off. You want the pizza or not, because if you don't I got two more deliveries to make. I can roll...

- No, no, no wait I think I have a few dollars somewhere.

Cracking the door open with her leg and the delivery dude peeping at it lustfully, she manages to find seventeen dollars in a drawer near her door and she pays him with all, even tipping him five dollars extra as he steps off.

Having found the history book with the initials scripted in the contents was enough to rattle him to a awakening clarity that feels impossible to bare. But his findings next out of all his inner suspicions away and it acknowledges his answers and place them right there in front of him. When he finds a vague pocket outside the bag that hangs a zipper. When he subdues inside he finds a picture that holds more words to him when he lays eyes on it.

DIANE slams the door and heads to the back room with the pizza in both hands curious and worried as to why DWAYNE never came like she asked. Blitzing through the door she finds him in the center of her bedroom facing adjacent in her direction holding a gun in his hand that catches her to resist moving any closer to him or movement period. Not understanding why and a bit fearing from his face she goes to ask him real carefully.

- I called you to the door for my purse and you never came. Why are you holding a gun like that in my room ?

She says to him paused in every muscle while continuing to hold the pizza in her jittery hands, real afraid at his stance.

DWAYNE there in the middle of the floor overlooking her with his face brutally delivering immediate death. Not missing a blink staring her down.

- I heard your call... and right in the middle when I grabbed your purse out your closet I found some shit that in this moment got me real fucked up and makes no sense to me seeing.

He says while before he ends she interrupts him.

- What you see ?

- SHUT UP, SHUT UP, SHUT THE FUCK UP RIGHT NOW DIANE. JUST SHUT UP FOR A MINUTE. And let me finish what I have to say...

DWAYNE screams at her as loud as he possibly can in a man tone.

Scared and trembling disbelief to him and his attitude that she's never been introduced to now, still with the pizza in her hands, she does what he says and listens.

- ...I found something in your closet and I'm going to ask you one question and all I want is one answer. Do you understand me ?

- Yes ?

She says swallowing hard in nervousness to the situation. DWAYNE marches over a few steps to her closet, reaches in and tosses out the gym bag on the floor for her to see looking down at it and asks her.

- I KNOW WHO THIS BAG BELONGED TO... AND SOMETHING IN ME TELLS ME THE FACT THAT YOU HAVING THIS BAG LET ME KNOW THAT YOU KNOW WHO IT BELONGED TO TOO... NOW WHAT I WANT TO KNOW IS...WHERE DID YOU GET THIS BAG FROM.

Standing there resembling froze listening and watching carefully to every word from DWAYNE'S mouth. DIANE frightened as can be waiting for him to finish his question so she wouldn't make the second mistake in interrupting him. Quickly hoping he wouldn't detect her as she hurries as best to summon a explanation to the question mentally, she turns her eyes away and down to the floor while her mouth blurts.

- I-I- I found it on the street not too far from here one night walking home.

A few steps ahead to her bold lie, expecting her to say what she says causes DWAYNE'S reaction like a tick when he fires a solid round from his pistol into her room door instantaneously near where she stands. The sound ringing out in shock disturbing fright that all in near perimeter had to have heard it and felt the distemper in the recoil. DIANE eyes shutter in panic as her body squirms in distress, her bare feet on the carpet floor without her knowing creep over in cringe to the other as if she's about to pee on herself . Shocking enough she still manages to grip tight the pizza in her hands as it juggles at the point of the shot.

- I ain't gotta tell you where the next one going.

She straightens up and confesses with ease.

- Alright, alright... I had just moved here and I didn't have a dime. There was this guy I met and he gave me his number and he asked me how did I feel about doing this job for him and it paid ten thousand dollars.

- What job ?

DWAYNE asks.

- The job was to attract this guy...this guy name ROBERT he told me... and that he wanted me to get this guy close to this address as possible, he didn't tell what he did or why, he just said get him to the place. If I did it I'd get five in the beginning and the other five once it was finished. I didn't know he was going to do what he did to the guy and I didn't even know he was just a little boy either.

- What else ?

DWAYNE demands.

- I led him to the place and he shot him.

- How'd you get the bag ?

- After he shot the boy, he swiped it and made me take it just in case I decided to switch up and start talking to the police after me knowing what he just did to him. The bag got my fingerprints on it. He made me leave and told me I'd get a call in two days and the person would tell me to be at a address. I got the call like he said and went to the address. I guess they expected me to go to the police because instead of the five I got fifty. That's how I got this place, and then met you...I love you DWAYNE.

DIANE confesses crying as tears stream fall down her face.

DWAYNE continuing to stare her down with his eyes filled with a tamed rage and his gun tightly gripped, reading her up and down standing there still holding the pizza. So he asks her while she remains whimpering.

- Your name really isn't DIANE is it.

- ...no, its...

He hushes her before she can say, not interested to even know. DWAYNE assimilates the direction of his previous desired question and moves back to his original questioning.

- The dude who gave you the job, what do you know about him. What he look like, name, address anything ?

- He's big, I mean real big. Brown skinned and tall. I never heard him use a name, I think on the card he gave me I remember him putting

RAZER, ROZIER, no it was RAZOR spelled exactly like the blade.

She informs detailing as much as she remembers confidently.

- Where he lived ?

- It was only a one time thing he never brought me to his place. Hold on...in my dresser over there, I have the address he told me to show up to. I wrote it down in my phone book under the address in case I forgot or I came up missing knowing what I knew. I remember it wasn't being that far from here on the bus ride at least eight, ten blocks away from here.

- Which dresser ? Top or bottom.

He asks.

- The top. It has a brown cover...

She tells.

Shivering in fear she stands there still with the pizza that's now about as cold as her after he's exhausted every question he sought to know from her in regards to the bag of his past. Peeping back at DWAYNE as he covers his face with no expression beaming dead at her and time passing in seconds that to her feels more like hours. Fuels her to question DWAYNE in the intensive peeping standoff between each of them.

- WHAT NOW !...

She says to him as he remains in his stance with his eyes leveled normal and his energy steaming for relentless violence uncaring of remorse or sympathy to her or anyone in the present element. The only empathizing thought that plagues DWAYNE'S mental state is him now coming into the factual knowledge involving a friend's crude murder that was too soon. Imagining the unbearable experience to be tricked and swindled by a female who's intentions was to guide you to your untimely death for a pathetic fee. Eyeing the treachery that bare face in front of him mingling with the haunting brainwork stored from the previous recollections builds fast, fast carrying a wind infused with vendetta at a non stop pace.

Still staring back at DWAYNE in his maniacal mode cringing her legs slightly more aggressively with her last question in subtly go without answer. Strengthens her a second round only this time crying agony.

- I have to pee !

After dropping her last syllable in her statement. Which she doesn't land the chance to hear once the trigger clicks and out the barrel sounds the disturbance wrecking a horrible loudness. The aiming fire from his gun pierce directly at her chest in single fours "BOOM, BOOM, BOOM BOOM", the impact in greatness sends her back first into the wall with the exiting bullets and blood leftover. She's down rearranged from the impact, and not bothered to use the bathroom any longer.

DWAYNE then raids her top dresser like she informed for the brown covered book enclosing the vital info listed. That he cant help to get his hands on with the tips of his fingers successfully when found.

He wastes no time in paying a trip to the residence that the paper from DIANE had saved to her phone log. Listing the address 5130 fourth street northeast, a apartment building. But it takes him a few days until he can put hands on "RAZOR" when he gets a close description of him sitting afar from a car peeping at all incomers and out-goers from the building. When in one day sitting there in the car as DIANE'S depiction confession ponders him to reminisce as he sees this dude exiting a green Monte Carlo holding true to her apparent on his way inside the building. But he wasn't for sure that the dude was indeed the person he was looking for. Cursing himself that he wished before killing DIANE that he asked her one last question which was "What car did he drive". As times moves on and the sun turns to night awaiting his departure from within the car running on straight emotion and adrenaline as chaser. DWAYNE them decides he can no longer resist the drive to overreact, he grabs his gun stuffs it into his hoody pocket and exits the car waltzing to the building's main entrance when he grabs the handle, exiting is no other than the man intending himself. Startled almost as he breezes by him making a disgruntled eye contact in passing. DWAYNE in his unexpected trance improvises quickly sneaking both hands into his pocket and as the guy stepping away he speaks out to him behind distant at the door.

- Ayy ! Don't they call you RAZOR.

The man right of way pauses in his path from walking and turns back around after his announcing without saying anything in response to the possible name claim. He marches boldly right back to the entrance door where DWAYNE stands as his shadow hover over him in force and brute power. Looking over DWAYNE being his physical state is much larger, once again making contact with his eyes in a demeanor suitable to the reputation of what was explained in DIANE'S explanation. There in his face, he then delivers his reply.

- Yea I'm RAZOR, who wanna know slim.

DWAYNE inattentive to a smudge of a second to pass from the intentional statement directed at him for intimidation to sink. Whips out his piece wrapped in both hands drawing it right between RAZOR'S eyes whispering his response in calm.

- He do !

After forcing him upstairs and back into his apartment. Naturally in size advantage RAZOR seeks his luck in controlling the situation by pursuing to take the gun. It doesn't work and he finds himself shot in his knee and his face bruised on account of DWAYNE'S brutal pistol play to his face for his challenging stunt. It isn't too bad though, he forced the giant to tell him everything that happened with ROCKET no different than his fall girl and who sent him out on orders. Who was running the show ? After the bullet to his knee there wasn't any need for further torturing because he gave everything up in exchange to keep his life. Pointing fingers in all directions bringing up MOISSON SERVICES. Then naming MOSS, ERNEST, and ALEX as the two main contributors to the boy's murder, confessing he was giving files with all their information inside from addresses, and their socials representing their case identification. Stating they were the orchestrators and he was merely only a henchmen carrying out duties that he was hired for. Scheming and plotting after hearing the whole ordeal, DWAYNE decides that he'll give RAZOR his freedom if he do one last thing for him. He makes him write a letter and closes it with ALEX'S social security number as a fear tactic. When finished DWAYNE keeps his promise alright...he keeps it a lie, blazing a bullet right through RAZOR'S head after him dropping the pin in his initial signature. In retaliation to him cutting up ROCKET the way he did, handy with a machete he gets a hold of. He dismembers his head from his shoulders. But being that his body was too heavy and more than gunshots heard from the apartment he felt removing the body would be too suspicious and even more a task to take on. So he wraps the body in plastic and stuffs it under the bed, then places the severed head in the closet.

Leaving both to hopefully be found by the police once the smell overbears the building at some point. DWAYNE proceeds on in undertaking his plot now appointed with more information that guides him to be more sinister in reaping righteousness in his revenge.

-- BACK IN THE ROOM SURROUNDED IN DARKNESS

Having be DWAYNE taking consideration in the last question asked by ERNEST. Shedding enlightenment on who he is, answers the mystery, fueling more heat to the flame.

- So that's how you stalked us.

ERNEST responds.

Still ALEX unveiling to DWAYNE with his arms behind him, progressive in his attempt before. He has now managed to free one of his hands with it remaining stretched behind him as he's fidgeting around with other with his wrist still confined in the cuffs. Doing the best he can to not give himself away in his escapist ploy, he dialogue as a distraction.

- That means nothing, how you know anything that RAZOR fucker said was true ? How absolutely positive you are that the file he gave you was grade A authentic ? And how you know he wasn't just fucking you around. I would, I would bullshit you or anyone else on some shit to make it seem real if my life was on the line.

ALEX comments.

Grinning in subtly to his explanation, DWAYNE smiles in ALEX'S face and then turns to ERNEST.

- That's true, true indeed. But I think to that you need to ask your father in sincerity and honesty as you possibly can. What's his connection to MOSS and MOISSON SERVICES. Matter fact won't you ask him man to man, son to son. How did he actually know MOSS ?

ALEX building up as much confidence as he can although his face exploits his uncertainty to the question based on DWAYNE'S obvious inside intel how he formatted it the way he did. Eyes intact he ejects.

- They're old school friends, right...dad.

ALEX states driven on accuracy. Asserting his head over in the direction after his response to his father who stares back at him as if his answer was flawed in proclaiming as well as obtaining.

- Very true ALEX, buddy, pal but there's more to the secret that you left out on. And I don't know about you but it would fuck me knowing this whole time my father wasn't one hundred percent in telling me something that could cost me my life. Especially when your in a ordeal like right now.

ALEX revolving his head in direction to his father, harboring validity to the lie.

- It was all a lie wasn't it, what else you've been keeping away from me and mom, dad. I knew you and Moss been cahoots since the day you gave me that card. But I didn't feel until now, that's the reason you never had the heart to tell me with even with us about to die right here and now in front of you. You know mom I realized in these last days of reckoning on my life something very important and tragic at the same time...

Mumbling words from his mouth directly at his father. ERNEST before not courageous enough to stare back at his son slightly turns his head and sees him squirming his hands free of the steel cuffs behind him, nearly dropping them to the floor before locking on to them.

- I realized how much a coward my father is. I bet even now with me saying this he doesn't even have the courage to tell me to my face. What is this big secret with MOISSON SERVICES now that you already in bed with them.

ERNEST focusing his radar over at ALEX with his hands free, the internal panic asks him what will he attempt to do next, whatever it is it won't be strategic only fatally foolish. Ignoring the question, ALEX poses to him. ERNEST looks over at DWAYNE standing there with DAISY on the floor eye to eye at him.

- We're all waiting ERNEST. Being honest won't kill you.

Lunging himself in flight as he possibly can from the chair restrained by the weight of the chains bearing his whole upper section. Arms stretched out in both directions like a butterfly as his son looks on, ALEX soars in at DWAYNE in hopes to take him down. But his idea in motion only seems to be achievable when in thought not in action. After his defying savior leap boosting in the air. Upping his tool in hand, DWAYNE thinks in reaction as ALEX looks to be coming at him, he blasts a round at him in jitters from being off guard to his move. It strikes him in the center to his torso breaking pass the metal snakes. The wounds relieves him of his momentum. ERNEST cries out "NO" as it echoes intermingling with the gunshot left ringing throughout the confined area. DAISY looks on with tears and everlasting moaning behind her gagging, frightened as ALEX body is halted in disfigurement by the shot that knocks him to floor hard.

Still conscious with his head poking up looking at the wound inconceivable to it and his in early regret to what has led him to the moment. DAISY straggles her way to him in a mom and medic fashion. Huffing and puffing in tears to the damage her son acquired before her. ERNEST looking on in a speechless outrage, his eye lids pressed back.

DWAYNE unwanted but now oblige to own up to finishing what he started. He looks over at ERNEST before stepping over, DAISY'S weeping mumbled cries scores the sorrow scene. ERNEST turns to DWAYNE as the lid on his eyes remain in shock at what he's done and carries on his looking, when he sees him cocking back the hammer for another round into the chamber. Walking over to ALEX, pulling DAISY away as she lays over him and his wound shed blood through his hands as he tries to nurse it in a messy pressure press that does no good. His mouth spurts blood as well. ERNEST gasping his last breath as millions of thoughts flash through him in seconds disabled in interfering. DWAYNE stands firm with his pistol aimed in close, DAISY screaming her head off after being tossed to the side like a rag doll, ERNEST stares in close shouting "PLEASE DON'T DO THIS". The sniveling he does isn't accomplishing, and doubtful if ever could be. As he stands over ALEX staring down at him, DWAYNE watches the fear in his face as he attempts to look away holding his hands like a shield hoping it circumvent the execution. He's wrong, DWAYNE pops a single shot into the top of his head that flat lines his arm blocking methods permanently. Across the room there's a scream " DADDY" from BRADY who stands from the chair he was seated in at the expense having to just watch his father be murdered before him. With his grandma screaming at his side.

DWAYNE turns to the boy with a look as they exchange a seconds worth of gazing at each other. It's clear in his expression he didn't want to attend to do what he did in viciousness in front of the boy. But what he did was necessary to be done. Interpreting as something other his internal, DWAYNE'S stares enforces the boy back into his seat. Turning away he looks over to ERNEST with his head down troubled. Acting fast when he finishes the dirty deed, he grabs DAISY from the floor as she bawls her eyes out on account of her son, witnessing his death in gore. DWAYNE forces her to the front of her bound husband. Seeing his head down angers DWAYNE and in fury he kicks his bloody wounded leg to bounce back into the scene. It dies behind his cries to the pain after the revival. Looking on does BRADY watching the commander with a gun and holding the scary object to his grandma's temple, hearing the sound of the trigger being pulled sounding almost as if a shell is cracking.

- LOOK AT ME...

Angrily DWAYNE tells ERNEST standing inches away from him cradling DAISY in his arms with his piece resting up against the side of her head. Feeling her breath and chest raise in and out accelerated in a beyond alarming shudder. Aligned to her irrefutable cries.

Basking in the pain from the kick, feeling the cool blood ooze in thick paste down his leg . ERNEST obeys the orders delivered and looks on at DWAYNE holding his traumatized, weeping wife with a gun to her head screened at his knees in the form of a theatre picture.

Displaying that his patience has been drained all this time. He devises one last cop out for ERNEST. No more talking, settling, or questions this is for real and all the mind games have ceased. He wants ERNEST to broadcast the truth out right there, and right now. If not, DAISY also tastes the same fate as her son just did minutes before and his body now resting in the pool of blood steps near. With a bullet through his body then a hole resting straight through the other side of his head.

- LOOK AT ME...then your son over there where I put him... Ok the same thing is going to happen to this bitch if you don't just tell her and all of us what we should all know from you. SAY IT... I'm a give you to the count of five and if I don't hear what I expect to hear, the next muthafuckin bullet I shoot is on you. Okay...go !

Hesitantly watching cringing his face as DWAYNE places the situation true context there before him. Seeming to still be reluctant in his commands. What he does, next delivers more pressure onto ERNEST and his decision making. He removes the cloth used to gag DAISY from her mouth and she screams the minute its off at ERNEST for him to help her. Begging him to reveal whatever it is for him to reveal that can dissolve her life from being in serious jeopardy ahead of his countdown.

- FIVE...

Removed to budging his face to resist making even the slightest move. Staring boldly at DAISY aching with her eyes wet from tears and her lower lip quake in fear having a gun held to her head. Feeling the warm tip of the barrel press hard up against the skin nearest to her ear. Unbearable knowing that her life is running on a short timer shedding away. Twitching her peripheral and primary sight toward the gun and back at ERNEST. Awaiting his consideration that's holding DWAYNE to a furious psychopathic expectancy.

- FOUR...

DWAYNE exclaims facing his vision directly towards ERNEST. Squinting deliberately rejecting any humor as he can only reciprocate the seriousness in the standoff with the aggressive energy building in pressure. Away from DWAYNE he turns to DAISY who's pleading countless to him to just make the message to whatever it pertains to known for her rescue that she believes. All the while disinclination not only plagues his thoughts in revealing but also his current state. DWAYNE staring him down holding his piece that doesn't even fidgets in his firm grip he goes in again to lock off another number closing in on the countdown to clashing.

- THREE...

DWAYNE calls.

- You watched while he killed your son and do nothing. You're willing to let him do the same to me to protect only yourself...what kind of a secret you have that is above the sake of your only family ERNEST.

He hears and it gives in to him to finally settle like desired.

- I don't know what you think I'd do, maybe I did and was fully aware to what MOISSON SERVICES is and what MOSS actually did.

- Bullshit and I should shoot you for saying dumb shit you knew exactly what was going on. Tell me why was ROCKET killed and I'll let your wife go right now. And that's two.

DWAYNE says. Meanwhile after stating his ultimatum at ERNEST, he pays close in observance to his hesitation that gives away a clue that most certainly he knows more than he's saying. He awaits in a short pause before responding.

- I don't fucking know, don't you think if I did I would tell you held up like this. Look what you did to my son.

He whimpers.

- It isn't like you care the way you beat him up back there at the car like that…yea that's right I saw that too.

DWAYNE replies. While ERNEST eyes light up in jolting surprise.

- Wait...where were you fighting ALEX ? ERNEST. Tell me...say it, say it right fucking now you goddamn coward.

DAISY interrupts.

- Tell her ERNEST, confess the truth....do it.

In a rage fit, shuffling around in all directions from forwards and backwards, stomping down and budging as hard as he can restricted by the chains. Calling for him to be set free avoiding the questions that are taking a toll on him that causes his overreaction.

- Look I've told you everything that I know. I don't know anything about a ROCKET or how he came about dying the way he did. Now please, please, please I've owned up to my end of the bargain, now you do the same motherfucker.

Gazing with a stare departing his reply to be anything of genuineness. DWAYNE releases from his tensed position and eases his piece down and then away from DAISY'S head leaving her stagger to the floor again. Holding himself to his words that he promised just as he said.

Relief showers DAISY'S face having the feeling she escaped her own death in close call, as she turns to ALEX body and makes herself over to him. ERNEST who's also grateful for her being out of his deadly grapple listens as DWAYNE speaks in a way as if this could be his last statement before granting them all exile.

- Ok…I can tell by this moment that there ain't nothing I can say or do to make you own up to being honest and I refuse to keep going on. But I do think I know how we can fix this.

Discouragement hits ERNEST in confusion to interpret what DWAYNE means in prior statement.

- Fix what ? What- what do you mean ?

He aims his gun over to DAISY, with ERNEST trailing his eyes as his trigger arm shift in her direction as she props herself beside ALEX'S expired body, streaming tears frantically. Clear to what's coming next, out ERNEST shouts in the deepest crave.

- NOOOO ! DAISY.

Acknowledging her name with a face filled with drops of everlasting grief. DAISY tilts her head up having to be caught in the moment unsettled to see her son dead and gone before her, and being helpless to the mercy of his killer. As she arises her intuition steers her in connection that flies pass ERNEST'S confined radar and directly to the frontal base of the gun that had recently been jammed up against her temple. Her heart delays in pulse, she blinks one time with grace, downing a swallow that sinks to bottom of her throat and wedges her lips apart for a muttered shriek. When it goes off twice tagging her once through the neck and chest she slings backwards dead in alignment angle to ALEX and his puddle of redness.

DWAYNE once its over with his revolver smoking harder than a cigar turns and outs one word at ERNEST in clear spite.

- That's one...

At the sound of the bullet ALEX'S son shutters in his skin at his seat peeping to the carnage being inflicted on his family one by one beginning first with his father now his grandmother. Although it's unwanted as he shield his ears flat with his palms calling with his gestures that the element is more than he can tolerate being a child.

ERNEST stricken to have to see his wife canceled out heartlessly. It flashing before his eyes almost like a train passing only him enraged as he screams out as loud as he possibly can "NOOOOO !". DWAYNE long away to anguish any concern to his action only stands there before ERNEST as he howls in his hurt. Clashing his weeping, DWAYNE interrupts firm.

- I don't have any sympathy for you man or your family so you can kill all that crying like I did your bitch. I made it clear to you before repeatedly to tell me the truth.

- I TOLD YOU TRUTH...

- YOU TOLD ME A BUNCH OF BULLSHIT THAT I SAW RIGHT THROUGH.

Defenseless in all degrees to humanity when removed from everything they loved. Almost everything, as DWAYNE speaks, ERNEST catches his glimpse to the left where his grandson sits burning his eyes at him nearly curled into a ball with his knees tucked into his chest. Wondering at the boy as his heart race fast from his inflaming panic, channeling his thoughts as words chanting for the boy to at least dare to run somewhere, anywhere before he has to witness his death which is now assured and could show up at any minute. BRADY doesn't latch on to the subliminal thinking, but DWAYNE does pick up on ERNEST and what holds his attention in his peripheral as he follows his eyes over to the boy. Before he can blaze his deep with intimidation at the boy like he's done before. He looks down at ERNEST and informs this.

- I'm a show you something.

He storms over to the boy's direction like a feared tyrant. ERNEST looking on feeling energy that could lead to the child being third in line to being victimized to his death. His eyes seeped wide unimaginable and with DWAYNE'S back facing him armored in black, he pictures gore like a psychic to come. Still bound in endless grips of chains and removed in heroism. ERNEST in dying rescue of his grandson recites the first thing that surface his mind in deflect.

- It was junior year at Wilhelm prep school. I made friends with this guy who had this odd idea...

Consuming his tone, DWAYNE pauses in his tracks then spins his head around as ERNEST'S monologue pours from him effortlessly stored in his memory. Deciphering his speech as it goes on, while ALEX'S son who's no more afraid listens on as he creeps past DWAYNE'S thick shadowy stature to even look on as he listens to his grandfather's wording like a fable to his ignorance.

- ...that evolved into a obsession. This infatuation how he thought he could make a forever ending economy from people and their...vital parts. Something that sounded beyond the imagination of a teenager. I tried time and time again to move him away on the idea but the more it seemed I tried to steer him another place. It just created his fixation to grow more and more. By our senior year he ended up sealing this plan in his year book for deeper motivation showing it to me, labeling it as his life's goal and it was clear to me by then he wouldn't stop at nothing until it came true. This friend I'm speaking about name was HORACE… HORACE MOSS. Once graduation we loss touch. Then after college I ran into him and he asks for a favor and before he could even hit me with the scheme. My mind had already informed me to what MOSS wanted, he had half but he needed more money to invest into his dream business. He needed more money, and the more money would lead to a partner. I didn't want to do it but something he said in that instance stayed with me, they were just a couple of words but I never forgot them and they claim hold to me this very instance now. He said "One day soon you'll need a favor" and he was right. I lent him my amount and sure enough my big day calling for that favoring came. And he paid me plenty from the success of his organ harvesting system. Targeting people from their stolen medical records if only and only if they fit a certain... appearance criteria he said.

- If they were black.

DWAYNE ousts over his storytelling.

- On account to all his research and all his eugenics theology and philosophy. Pointed to the sufficient genetic conclusion that melanin inclined people anatomy was much efficient and dominant in the case to those who weren't. Melanoid's as MOSS called them were strengthen from source of the sun which naturally energized them from within as well as without. We're talking human photosynthesis where you have a group of people who have the ability to recharge themselves of any poison or negativity involved with their vessel just by simply stepping outside into the sun. The more darker in hue, the greater domination melanin took affect. And the younger maturity peak in elusiveness, MOSS took this beautiful intelligence and used it to his deranged advantage in support for abundance of his pricey clients who suffered in opposite of people who are melanin inclined. Ninety percent of black children missing, never to be seen again through out the years stuck in cold cases even adults here in this city all result from MOISSON SERVICES. Now you wanted a explanation for your friends abduction and murder. There it is, you still think you can handle what's really going out there in that bag of tricks you call a society and beloved country.

Listening without responding a word. DWAYNE redirects himself back into the vicinity of the young boy. ERNEST hinting easily from the gesture he's wasn't convinced by him conversing straight forward so he countered his confession with his earlier intentions in harm. So he shrieks with bursting out "NOOOO". DWAYNE never lays a hand on the boy instead in his back facing position on cue after ERNEST'S worry. A switching sound blares through the room and all at once the room glows in a single brightening glare in fluorescence aiming above. The shock of the radiance in lights steers ERNEST into winging himself as much as he can around picturing the room that was once covered into total darkness now basking in emptying luminance.

About face now with his index finger tipping the switch that set on in the room upward is DWAYNE beside the boy who also doesn't resist to blinking his eyes hectic for a moment from the gloom to glow. There's a table behind the boy and on it propped up ERNEST notices multiple machinery devices accompanied with a television that couldn't be no more than thirty inches. Not settled to realizing what's going on, DWAYNE wastes no time into explaining to him.

- What is this ?

ERNEST asks.

- Look real close here and its ok if you want to smile.

DWAYNE replies while pointing at one of the machines propped on the sturdy table top.

- What is that ? And what are you talking about ?

Removing his finger from the switch DWAYNE presses a button slightly below the screen of the television for it's connection. When the screen emerges ERNEST views himself before it from life to picture. Glaring at himself constrained and barred with chains. DWAYNE quickly explains the disposition.

- It took a while for what I wanted to hear but at least we'll give the audience a show while they waited. You know.

Coated in overwhelm and discharging his infuriation as the chains rattle in noise rumbling away around ERNEST jolting himself side to side causing commotion. As he roars in speech to him being coerced by DWAYNE deceptively while being recorded.

- COCK-FUCKING SUCKER you tricked me. You roped me into talking just for this shit.

ERNEST explodes in obscenities.

- A trick is a deception. Me taking out that bitch of yours and son was just icing on the cake. But this here...this here is my payback...Tell me something do you know what it feels to have someone who had high hopes and dreams snatched from you ? Have you ever saw a mother weep in faint when she has to go to the coroners office to identify her son's body after it was shredded open and left behind in a garbage bin like a empty coke bottle or a rotten banana peel some muthafucka just threw away like candy paper ? Have you ever had to read a newspaper articles where the journalist constantly highlights the potential and what that person could've been if they were still here? Muriel's that hold nothing but reminders to the pain that you experienced in that one moment you found out that someone you loved was gone?

DWAYNE states with empathizing feeling.

- I told you everything I fucking know you black-nigger-piece of shit.Your bucket shooting friend is fucking dead, and you carrying on like his little weeping bitch with a vengeance ain't gonna bring him back either. Now kill me or let me out these fuckin' chains NOOOW !

ERNEST tones enraged.

Calm to his overtop antics filled with meanness. DWAYNE as chill as can be carries into one last question that coincides with his previous statement.

- Or have you ever felt the satisfaction in putting a bullet straight through the skull of the muthafucka who killed your BROTHER ?... I can !

DWAYNE doesn't even waste a one breath for him to reply before he puts his gun into his mouth and unload simultaneously three times. ALEX'S young son eyes widen in surprise when it undergoes.

When DWAYNE finishes he ejects two tapes from the two recorders there on the top side by the television. Stuffing one into his coat with the other flat on the table. He turns to the boy who will most certainly after this experience will forever be mortified and stares at him while he does the same in return. It takes a while as the boy just looks on at DWAYNE, knowing that his gory and grisly departure is there before him as DWAYNE lifts his piece with his barrel upward. The boy drenched in the most fear his body can take doesn't program to make one move. From the crack of both his eyes rains, DWAYNE watches emptying the chamber of his gun that's spilled every shell. He pockets the piece behind his back. Then walks over to the boy looking him face to face before assuring he would not hurt him.

He cradles the boy in his arms as he exits from the room accomplishing in rewarding requital.

At a doorstep in broad light of day holding the boy no different before, DWAYNE slowly and carefully puts the boy on the ground as he stares. DWAYNE gives a few knocks to the door, then leaves the little boy as he speedily just walks away. The boy turns and looks at him before a voice from the door arose belated coming. When it opens there's an older women mature in age and complexion dark full of peace. The boy turning away as DWAYNE had already made himself up the street from the tick of the engine then to the women speechless to this unsuspecting finding curious in excitement.

- Oh my god...hi honey where's-where's your mother ?

The boy standing there spinning his sight all over from the street where it was once visible to see the vehicle DWAYNE abandoned him with . Unsure about anything at the moment the boy clinching his hand around his toy doesn't respond to the concerned woman in essence of kindness.

She improvises next in the questioning.

- What about your dad ? You know where your daddy is ? Hmmm baby.

She asks carefully.

Continuing to still feel incoherent to her personal examination. The boy nearly doesn't reply to her inquire with what all has happened and he's seen. His passive attitude is removed from guard when he stops and stares at the woman and she flashes him a smile. Instinctively connecting to him that everything's going to he fine to this point. Which comforts him to speak.

- He's dead.

The boy manages to say.

The older woman reacts disheartening to the boys response.

So as she stretches out her hand for his invitation inside the boy looks at her hand that reminisces his trust that led to the previous massacre he's witnessed with DWAYNE. He then spots the woman's smile again matching it in similarity to his own mom that renders in his thoughts. He joins his hand with hers and steps inside to the woman's home and she shuts the door with her last words stating "Lets see if we can find your mother, do you have a name ?"

Attaching one hand over the steering wheel soft moving at the pace of the street filled with countless drivers all in row moving from one light to the next. The heavy flow in traffic is at peace with the breezy night air. Down he rolls the window to catch a feel for himself, he feels his past pain and hurt allured. It withers away almost like waste. A good sensation overcomes with a pat on his back in just physical illusion but supernaturally authentic that reassures him spiritually where it derives. Coming to a red, DWAYNE reaches to the rear seat behind him and jams the old bag from DIANE'S closet to his lap. He unzips the vault and retrieves something in a important remembrance to him. A photo in his hands that calls for him to peep at in proudness and esteem before the street signal switches color.

In it captures a brief flashing memory having himself side by ROCKET. Smiling clinching hands solid like a fist as long lost comrades, or more like real BLOOD BROTHERS from the same mother and father sharing split semblance in looks which alludes this conclusion after the label scripted below the friendly image in words stating must've been written by ROCKET in some time stating "Me and Big Brotha". Still eyes front at the picture, he can hear ROCKET'S voice echoing the statement in validity which brings him to a comforting settlement. So he pins the photo next to his speed odometer.

Away from DWAYNE'S breath of ease spins to the police taping the room where ERNEST and his family are found in a chilling dread. A portrait splashed in a boundless terror, with three bodies horrifically murdered. Gagged, beaten, suffered, and then killed. A intriguingly plot for the front page of a global article to feed as a reminder to the masses to maintain their fear in this realm of the western world. Detectives roam the space for clues and hints belonging to the maniacal culprit, when a uniform so happened to pass the table where a photographer flashes photos for evidence. The light deterring him forcing for a head turn where he ends in seeing the tape there on the table left behind for his inspection. He grows even more to the tape and contents held on it when he also uncovers the propped machines being accessible to the act in playback. In his next move he calls over for assistance in his findings.

Meanwhile DWAYNE cruises loose down the road leaving behind him all burdens on his soul even altering his appearance unrecognizably to his former guise. Pursuing highway pavement out of town. His relief soothes him deeper for a smile after a glimpse down at the photo neighbor to the odometer where a uplifting reminder with multiple emotions rest. He gains acceleration and off he pushes in outer darkness being veiled from rampant red rear lights surfacing all over.

THE END

www.ingramcontent.com/pod-product-compliance
Lightning Source LLC
Chambersburg PA
CBHW080018130626

46556CB00016B/3224